Forever Girl

Forever Girl

Sherry Ann Fortner

ETSI PUBLISHING GROUP
ATLANTA, GEORGIA

Etsi Publishing Group
For details write Manager of Sales
3420 Millwater Crossing, Atlanta, GA 30019

First edition October,2014

The characters and events portrayed in this book are
fictitious. Any similarity to real persons, living or
dead, is coincidental and not intended by the author.

ISBN-978-0-9960745-0-6

Printed in the United States of America

꧁Forever Girl is dedicated꧂ . . .

to my daughter, Jennifer Harper, for her design of my website, the covers of my books, and for always asking if there's anything else I need her to do.

His legs *are as* pillars of alabaster, set upon sockets of fine gold: his countenance *is* as Lebanon, excellent as the cedars. His mouth *is* most sweet: yea, he *is* altogether lovely. This *is* my beloved, and this *is* my friend

Song of Solomon 5:15-16

℘1.GUILT

I RAN FOR ONLY A FEW YARDS WHEN I SUDDENLY stopped. Annie, how could I leave her there with that . . . that thing? Undecided, I stood there. I loved Annie. Annie seemed fond of me too, but she had commitment issues. I wrote it off due to her losing her mother at such an early age. Even though I've never stopped humping other girls, Annie is the only one I've ever wanted. The others were just for kicks. She is the girl that I am determined to have in the end. I was sure that eventually she would come around and give into me, but then he came. Ever since that new guy, Zell, started school at Mill Creek, she has not given me the time of day. I wanted to make her pay for ignoring me. I wanted to make her pay for dropping me and giving Zell all her attention. I wanted to make them both pay for the humiliation that I felt in the cafeteria. I made it clear to the guys at school that Annie was exclusively mine. I had so thoroughly terrorized them that no guy dared to speak to Annie for more than a few minutes.

Then, Zell showed up, and he couldn't be intimidated. Every time I confronted Zell, he stood up to me. He silently dared me to continue. I knew Zell would pursue Annie if he wanted, and there was nothing I could do about it. If I stepped over the line with Zell, I knew there would be a fight. I enjoyed a rumble now and then but not one I couldn't win. I didn't think I could win a fair fight with Zell; though, I had nothing to give me that feeling but instinct. Something about that guy was different. He exuded an aura of perpetual danger.

I loved Annie, yet I had left her there for a monster to tear to shreds. Would Zell have left her? Somehow, I didn't think so, and the thought shamed me.

What is that thing? The beast is several feet taller than me. I am a tenacious force myself at six feet, three inches and two hundred twenty pounds of muscle, but when compared to that creature, I am insignificant. Fingers of panic and remorse grabbed at my chest. I couldn't leave Annie. I started back toward the sound of her scream. I'd just made it back to her when I saw the creature had her in its grasp. I thought the creature might have been a large bear, but this thing that had Annie was no bear. It was a hairy mountain with long, sharp teeth. I have fished and hunted these woods since I was a young boy. There has never been reports of a creature like this. One thing that I was sure about, this was not a natural creature but a supernatural one. This was a monster from the pit of hell.

As I stood helpless, trying to figure out how to distract the monster, another creature swooped from the sky and scooped Annie right from the mouth of the beast. The beast tried to clamp its jaws down on Annie to prevent her escape, but its enormous fangs just ripped through the flesh of her legs as if they were butter when the being tore her from its jaws. The great beast stood on its hind legs and screamed into the night. I covered my ears. The sound terrified me.

What creature was this that had Annie now? I knew it had wings, but it dropped from the sky so swiftly and snatched her so quickly that it took me and the beast by surprise. I disappeared behind a tree and leaned against it. Where was Annie? The thing that snatched her had great wings and was amazingly huge, but it had the form of a man—of that I was sure. Had the creature saved her, or was she in even more danger? For all I knew, the second creature may have already killed Annie. What was it people say when something like this happened? Out of the frying pan and into the fire? The monster was still roaring and screaming. I was trembling. I climbed into the midst of some vegetation that was growing rampant between several trees. I curled into a ball and waited there for the monster to stop screeching and leave.

I was filled with remorse. This is all my fault. Annie's blood was on my hands. I brought her here. I'm sure she is dead, and I made her last hours alive horrific. I kidnapped her, threw her in my truck, and brought her to our family cabin in the woods. She escaped and ran from me when I drove to the nearest store for supplies. I kidnapped her in a jealous rage, and I hadn't planned this well at all. When we arrived at the cabin, there was nothing to eat or drink. I didn't plan on letting her go anytime soon, and that made a trip to the store a necessity. I planned on keeping her until I was ready to let her go, and that wouldn't be until she was in love with me. I was going to make her love me. After all, I'm Jonathan Howard, Mill Creek High School's star athlete, and girls fall in love with me daily. Why should Annie be any different? She will be mine and mine alone before I take her back. She will forget all about Zell. He will not want her anyway when I finish revealing to him all the intimate details about our nights alone in the cabin. Zell will hate her, and that is what I want.

I can't help thinking of Annie. She is gorgeous. The most beautiful thing about her is that she doesn't realize how beautiful she is. Her blond hair falls to her waist, and her big, blue eyes are always smiling. She has a peaceful spirit about her that is the opposite of my tumultuous one. She is slim yet perfectly built, and I decided in seventh grade that I had to have her. I pursued her all through middle school and high school. Then, *he* came. I was so consumed with jealousy that I never considered what would happen to me if somehow, Annie freed herself and went to the police. Blindly, I believed that if she were alone with me, she would forget all about Zell. Now, she's gone, and I'll never see her again. I put my head in my hands and began to weep silently. It was then that I heard the snapping of twigs and branches all around me. I shook violently. Was the creature still here? Was it looking for me? Were there more of them? I held my breath and waited. I could barely control the violent shaking that overtook me. I had to control it, or the monster would find me. The beast roared and screamed again only feet from the brush where I was hiding.

❧2.Zell

FOR THE FIRST TIME IN MY INTERMINABLE LIFE, I panicked. I held Annie with one arm tenderly as I flew, and with the other hand, I tilted her chin upward and back. Carefully, I blew into her mouth not wanting her lungs to explode with my strength. All the way to the hospital, I alternately blew gently into her mouth, compressed her chest, and tried to stem the great sobs which rumbled within me. My tears wet her face and drenched her hair, but I could not control the sorrow that ebbed out of me like an uncontrollable tide. It felt as though a six thousand year old dam inside me burst. I could not stop the waves of pain that rolled through me. Fighting to control my emotions, I landed just out of sight of the hospital entrance. Transforming back to Zell Starr, I strode toward the emergency entrance with her lifeless body cradled in my arms. I gave no thought to the fact that my jeans were ripped apart from the thigh down. I tore my tattered shirt from me and tossed it and my swords in some shrubbery as I carried Annie through the wide emergency room doors..

"Help me!" I thundered walking into the waiting room. "She's been attacked by an animal." Two nurses came out from around the desk, and when they saw Annie's lifeless face immediately called a code blue emergency. They attempted to take her from me, but I could not turn her loose.

"Please, the older nurse urged, "we can't help her while she is still in your arms."

I bent my head and pressed my lips to hers willing her to live. My eyes were awash with tears as I met the gaze of the nurse. "Save her," I pleaded.

"We're going to do everything possible to save her. I promise you," the nurse whispered as she peeled Annie from my grasp. Silently, two burly men appeared with a stretcher. Tenderly, they laid Annie on it and pushed her immediately through a wide door which closed soundlessly behind them. I saw a team of doctors and nurses waiting just beyond the door.

"Young man," the nurse turned back to me, "we need some information on the girl." I could not tear my eyes from the door. My beloved was there just beyond them. Death hovered making it hard to breath. I could do nothing to bring her back—to save her.

"Sir," the nurse tried again laying a hand gently on my arm.

I tore my gaze from the door and looked at her with tortured eyes. She guided me toward a computer. As soon as I finished giving the attendant Annie's name and the name and number of her father, I backed slowly toward the door and stepped outside. I retrieved my shirt and swords from their hiding place and moved around the corner of the building and snapped my wings into place. I returned only ten minutes later with my tattered and torn garments replaced with Annie's favorite gray jeans and shirt. Annie's frantic father ran through the hospital door as I stood at a window trying to control the sorrow which completely and utterly held me in its grim embrace. Frantically, his eyes searched the emergency room lobby. I could see relief spread across his taunt face when he saw me.

"Zell, what has happened to Annie?"

"She was attacked by some sort of creature. She called me from the lake and asked me to come get her. When I arrived, she was in the state that she is in now. I think she died on the way to the hospital. I gave her CPR, but I don't know. I don't know if they were able to bring her back." My anguished voice broke, and I had to stop.

Dr. Hayes rushed to the desk area in the lobby.

"Where is my daughter?" he shouted.

"She is with the trauma team. She is in very good hands. Our trauma unit is one of the best in the country. Don't give up hope. One of the doctors will let us know something as soon as possible."

Dr. Hayes and I waited for over an hour. Mumbling, Dr. Hayes paced the floor. I knew he prayed for Annie's life to be spared. Feeling worthless and not fit to pray, I stood by a window and looked out into the night. I had a beast to find and kill, but I will not leave Annie while there is still a slim chance that she will live.

Dr. Hayes had taken a seat and sat with his hands holding his head. I moved toward him hoping to comfort him.

"Dr. Hayes?"

He lifted his head in response and a faint smile crossed his face.

"Sit down beside me, son."

"I'm so incredibly sorry. I love Annie more than life itself. I should have prevented this."

"I know you would give your life for Annie. That thought comforts me greatly. I am so thankful she has a friend like you." Dr. Hayes patted my hand and looked into the distance.

"I mean it. If Annie lives, you may have to adopt me. I don't know if I can ever leave her side again."

Dr. Hayes gave a low chuckle which gave way to sobs.

"I can't go through this again. She is such a ray of sunshine. She is the one thing that I love more than life itself too. She's my baby."

I grasped Annie's dad's hands which he held clutched at his knees. I laid my forehead against his bent head while we both wept softly.

For hours, we huddled together waiting. Finally, an exhausted doctor came through the same door that Annie disappeared behind.

"Dr. Hayes." The doctor seemed to know Annie's father and held out her hand.

"Yes, Dr. Newman. How is my daughter?"

"We were able to bring her back though just barely. She is in a coma. She is stable at the moment, though very seriously ill. We have run a series of tests on her. We should have some results back soon. The trauma team has worked feverishly, and we will continue to treat her throughout the night. She has a severe laceration on her thigh that we think was inflicted by some sort of animal. We have tried several anti-venom antidotes for several predators that are native to this area. Nothing has worked. We have started her on an extremely strong antibiotic. There could be a bacterial infection from the saliva of the creature that attacked her. Do you have any idea what it was?"

Dr. Hayes looked at me.

"It was a huge beast, but I cannot tell you what kind. It was very dark. I just grabbed Annie and headed for the hospital."

"You probably saved her life—for now." Dr. Newman turned to face Annie's father again. "Reverend, I've got to be honest with you. This is serious. Prepare yourself for the worst. I've never seen a patient as sick as Annie pull through. We will wait for her test results before discussing options, but I want you to know that Annie's chances are extremely slim."

"May we see her?" Dr. Hayes asked.

"You may come in for a few minutes." The doctor motioned for us to follow her through the door.

Annie clung tenaciously to life. Annie's father insisted that we be allowed to stay in the room. He knew almost everyone in the hospital since he was there almost daily checking on members of his congregation, and he assisted anyone else that wanted spiritual advice at the hospital. We watched while Annie lay unconscious in a hospital bed while a fever raged within her. The venom from the monster attacked her body. The doctors were puzzled as to what sort of creature had attacked her and were unsure of how to treat Annie. They had tried several protocols, but still her fever raged. They also acknowledged that it may be a bacterial infection from the salvia of the predator's bite and were treating her with strong antibiotics. Her father sat beside the bed holding her hand with his head bowed in prayer.

As I watched her, I thought back to my first vision of Annie. She was like a distant star, dazzling, yet she was more real than anything I had ever known. Before she was even born, she was my sanctuary. Whenever the nights were dark and lonely, I would think of her, and she would turn nightfall to midday. I longed for her breath on my face, to smell her hair, her scent. I was perpetually homesick for her for millenniums.

I thought back to the first time I gazed into her face. It was the day she was born. I arrived while her mother was still in labor. Drawn by some unexplained force, I traveled across several continents as her mother's time neared. Though I first loved her in that vision when I was fourteen, nothing can be said for the love I felt for her the first time I saw her in the hospital nursery only minutes after her birth. I have never been far from Annie's side since. Annie's mother thought she was the most perfect baby ever born sleeping through the night from the day of her birth. Little did she know, it was I who cared for her during the night. It was the first real joy I had ever experienced in six thousand years of life when I held her sleeping in my arms. I have always protected mankind from evil throughout the years of my existence, but when I held Annie on that first night, I knew I would give my life for her.

As she grew into a precocious toddler with big blue eyes and blonde curls framing her angelic face, I was smitten. Just days after Annie was born, I battled the first Dark One that came for her. I never felt such rage. I made shambles of the creature that was foolish enough to steal into her room that night. I really made a mess, and I spent the next several hours cleaning up the splattered Dark One. Through it all, Annie slept peacefully. Her parents never knew how close she came to death. It was several years before the next one came. A vampire demon had tried to get to Annie while her mother was driving to church one night. Annie's mother struggled with the vampire. The vamp ripped her throat out, and the car crashed throwing Annie from her car seat. I tried to save them both, but when Annie was thrown from the car, I had to make a decision. The only decision I could make was to save Annie. I knew if I had time to ask her mother, her mother would have wanted her daughter's life's spared instead of her own. With that thought, it eased the guilt and responsibility I felt for Annie's mother's death somewhat but did not erase it.

A couple of years later, a Dark One laid in wait for Annie as she returned home just after dark from playing with her friend next door. I stepped between them, bent down, and whispered to Annie to run to her father. Annie did just that. I had just finished incinerating the latest creature when Annie came back out the door pulling her father behind her. Dr. Hayes saw me for a brief moment in my full Anak manifestation: alabaster face, wings erect, and a sword in each hand dripping with the blood of a dark creature. Dr. Hayes fell to his knees believing he had just witnessed the appearance of an angel. That event dramatically changed his life, and that is when Dr. Hayes left his scientist position for the ministry. Even though I am sure Dr. Hayes still remembers the moment, I do not think that he recognizes me as the angelic being standing beside a burning, stinking mound in his yard. Annie doesn't remember the attack. She still does not remember any encounters with me or the Dark Ones from her childhood to this day. That is how I want it. I do not want her frightened to live her life. Yet I know from standing guard every night since her birth, she remembers me and the Dark Ones in her dreams and nightmares.

After that, the attacks came on a yearly basis. Recently, since the night in the parking lot, the attacks have become more frequent. They're occurring every few days. Annie is older now and closer to my age as far as appearances go. I decided that it is time she knew. It is time Annie realizes the inevitable path her life will take, and she recognizes the forces out there which are poised to kill her. Evidently, the Dark Ones know her time of destiny is close at hand because of their broadened attacks. Uneasy due to the heightened attacks, I enrolled in her high school. The Dark Ones' attacks were intensifying. I needed to be close to her at all times. Even though Annie, her classmates, and her father have accepted me as a fixture in their lives, Annie still manages to open herself to danger.

Now, as she lay in the hospital bed fighting for her life, I was unable to cope with the thought that she may die again. This time it was my fault. I should have not left her at school unguarded. I had only thought to be a few hours. I waited until she was safely at school before I left. I thought that I would be back before basketball practice was over. I did not account for the jealously of Jon. I could have waited until the weekend and taken her with me to my mountain top facility in Switzerland. All of Starr Knives and Swords are made the old-fashioned way—by hand. I wanted to personally make Annie a weapon to hold off anything that might attack her until I could reach her. I became obsessed as I worked making her weapon a work of art unlike anything that has ever been made before.

Annie has a stubborn, independent nature, and she was not sold on the idea of a bodyguard. I worried about her. Three times now, I was almost too late. Of one thing I was sure, if Annie died, I would be next. It was one thing to have a vision of her and patiently wait for her throughout millennium, but now that I had touched her and fallen hopelessly in love with her, I would not live without her again.

If she dies, Annie has an eternal soul. But I was Annunaki. Did the Annunaki have souls? I thought not. My father was a fallen angel. Angels were not a human creation; they were not one of the redeemed. They were of a different order. Which order was I? Soulless like my father, or did I have a soul like my mother? I was sure that I was soulless, or if I did have a soul, it was blackened by the blood of my father. I was eternal like my father, wasn't I? I have lived for thousands of years. Humans after the flood, were only allotted up to one hundred twenty years. Therefore, if Annie dies, her eternal soul will live on, but I, without a soul, cannot follow her to where she is going. Yet no matter what torment awaits me, if Annie dies without the prospect of me following her into eternity, I will hunt the Dark Ones and viciously kill them all. I will kill all but the final one just as I had done in the days of old with the Anak. Finally, I will allow the last one of them to end it for me.

Tears welled up in my eyes clouding my vision as I watched her labored breathing. Emotion saturated my chest cutting off my breath. She looked almost ethereal lying there. Her face was flushed with fever and damp strands of her hair clung to her forehead and cheeks. Her long, dark eyelashes fluttered. Was she dreaming? Was she dreaming of me or the horrible monsters that hunted her? If she pulled through this, would I be able to protect her as she set about fulfilling her destiny? I love her beyond reason, and the thought of anything harming her filled me with such rage that I could scarcely contain it. I felt powerless to help her now as she fought for her life. Attempting to will her back to health, I clung to her hand.

"Dr. Hayes?" A distinguished looking man in a white coat slipped into the room quietly and addressed Annie's father.

"Yes," Dr. Hayes answered.

"I am Dr. Patel," the man began. "I have some news concerning your daughter's condition. Annie has a serious medical condition, Sepsis, commonly characterized by a whole-body inflammatory state, and the presence of a suspected infection. As you know, we have been using an antibiotic therapy, which has not given satisfactory results. We can treat Sepsis with a blood transfusion. However, Annie has a very rare blood type, of which, I am sure you are aware. Her blood type is outside of the ABO blood typing system. The National Blood Bank does not even have a supply of this blood. There are only two other known persons in North America with this blood type, a brother and sister in Massachusetts. The hospital staff is aware that your late wife was a first cousin to the couple in Massachusetts, and Annie also carries the blood type. It is called Bombay Blood (subtype h-h). It is called Bombay Blood only because that is the city in which it was first typed. We will attempt to contact that couple to see about a possible donation. Without such a donation, Annie will not survive. In fact, Annie may not even have time for us to fly the blood in. She may have only hours . . . minutes."

"That is not necessary, Doctor," I said, rising to my feet. "I can give Annie the blood she needs." I had not thought there was any way that I could help Annie, but if a blood transfusion could save her life. I could save her.

Both Dr. Hayes and Dr. Patel paled as their jaws went slack in astonishment.

"How is this possible?" Dr. Patel asked. "Are you a relative?"

"No, but I assure you that my blood is a match for Annie." I was not sure what type of blood I have, but I know it is an eternal blood. I saved another's life in the years since the invention of blood transfusions. My blood will not be rejected by Annie's body, and my ancient blood will actually heal her. Of that, I am sure. I began to have hope.

"Bombay blood does not contain ABO blood group antigens; therefore, Annie cannot receive a transfusion but from persons with the Bombay blood type. A transfusion that is not Bombay blood will kill her."

"My blood will heal her."

Well, um, it will do no harm to test it," Dr. Patel stuttered quite unnerved and shocked by my disclosure. "Can you follow me to the lab? We need to run some tests." Doctor Patel moved to the door.

"No, Doctor, I'm sorry. You will have to send the lab to me. I will not leave this room," I stated as politely as possible.

"Is there a reason you cannot walk down to the lab?"

"Yes, I must stay with Annie. I cannot leave her for any reason. She is in the condition that she is now because I left her. I will not do it again."

Sherry Fortner

"I'll see what I can do. We are preparing to move Annie to ICU, A team will be here shortly to transport her," Dr. Patel asserted wrinkling his brow and hurrying from the room.

Only a few minutes passed before a shaken, bespectacled, blood technician with spiky hair hurried into the room. I sat down in a chair beside Annie's bed.

"Well, now, holy cow, I've never seen such a muscular arm before. I hope my needle will pierce it," the technician gave a snort and mumbled nervously looking at me and shrinking back from me at the same time obviously unnerved by my size and stature. The technician tried to wrap a rubber hose around my arm just above the elbow. He became even more frustrated because it was too short and would not encircle my arm. He ended up tying two rubber hoses together to wrap around my arm. Inserting a needle into a vein, he withdrew several vials of blood from me before withdrawing the needle. He covered the puncture site with a bandage and hurried from the room adjusting his spectacles on his perspiring nose without another word.

"Thank you," Dr. Hayes moved to pat my arm.

"I would give my life in exchange for hers," I replied never taking my eyes from Annie.

"Thank you, son, you will have my eternal debt if you can save my daughter."

At the word son, I tore my eyes from Annie's face and looked into her father's eyes. "No one has ever called me son before, and you have done so twice this evening."

"Where is your father? Did he never call you son?"

"I have no idea if my father even exists anymore."

I could tell by the look on Dr. Hayes' face that he thought my response was a strange way to say that my father may be deceased. Dr. Hayes patted my shoulder.

"From this day forward, you consider Annie and me your family."

"Thank you, sir. You cannot imagine how your offer to be included in your family overwhelms me," I felt my eyes flash with emotion.

I reached over to cover Annie's small, fragile hand again with my own.

"I should have not allowed this to happen."

"Don't blame yourself. You were not with her when this occurred."

"That is precisely my point. I should have been. I shouldn't have let her out of my sight," my voice broke as I answered Dr. Hayes.

"Don't blame yourself. Annie is not your responsibility," Dr. Hayes replied, resting a hand on my shoulder.

"She is my responsibility, my destiny, and my life," I whispered. Dr. Hayes looked puzzled. He acted as though he was not sure he had heard me correctly.

Abruptly, I rose and walked to the window looking into the night. The technician was probably typing my blood right now and discovering that it was unknown. I hoped this revelation would not bring the medical community down upon me making me a freak show, but it was a risk I was prepared to face for Annie. I steeled myself for a fight because I am sure the doctor will not want to use me for a transfusion when he receives the lab report.

Within thirty minutes of the technician leaving the room, the door opened, and the room filled with doctors. Every doctor on duty in the hospital must have filed into that room filling it with white coats, and that sea of white coats stood against the wall staring at me.

"Young man, what is your name?" A nervous Dr. Patel asked.

"Zell Starr," I answered quietly.

"Have you ever donated blood before?" Dr. Patel asked him.

"Yes," I answered giving no additional information.

"And what happened?" Another doctor asked.

"The patient recovered."

"Where did this transfusion take place?"

"In Europe."

Dr. Patel cleared his throat. "Do you know your blood type is unknown to us?"

"I thought it might be," I answered.

"Why did you think that?"

"I had this same conversation when I tried to give blood in Europe to save a friend's life."

"What type of blood did this friend have?"

"I'm not sure." I said, moving over to the bed and taking Annie's hand. "All I know is that my blood seems to be compatible with any blood type."

"I'm sorry to say that we cannot use you for a donor," Dr. Patel replied.

"Test it. I know what I am talking about. Annie's body will not reject my blood. It will heal her. You said yourself she is dying. She may only have minutes. You cannot fly to Massachusetts, take a donor's blood, even if you can contact them and have them waiting, fly the blood back, and have enough time to save Annie," I argued. I could fly there faster, but that will mean Annie will be alone and defenseless while I am away. My best option is to convince these doctors to perform the transfusion.

"Tell them Dr. Hayes. Tell them to do it. Tell them to save Annie's life," I begged Annie's father. "I wouldn't do anything to harm Annie, and you know it. I can save her Dr. Hayes. I can save her," my voice broke with emotion.

"I don't know if I can take that chance. Perhaps, we need to try for the couple in Massachusetts," Dr. Hayes said sadly.

"Dr. Hayes could I speak with you in the hall privately for a moment?" I asked. Dr. Hayes nodded and followed me through the wide door into the hallway. The doctors began to gather together in clumps discussing the information that I had disclosed.

"Dr. Hayes I can't tell you everything about me, but I have come here to protect Annie. I have been protecting her for many years." With that revelation, he examined me. I could see that he was frightened. I knew he wondered how I could have been protecting Annie for several years. He thought me to be a teenager, and he had never even seen me until a couple of weeks ago.

"What do you mean?" he asked, taking a step back from me.

"Do you believe in eternal beings, angels, demons, and such?" I pushed him for an answer.

"I'm a pastor, of course I do," he answered paling.

"Then believe that my blood will heal her. You heard the doctor say there was no known type for my blood," I stopped waiting for an answer from Annie's father.

"Yes, I heard that."

"Then believe that the blood that runs through my veins is an eternal blood, a healing blood, which can save your daughter." Dr. Hayes looked faint and seemed to sway before me.

"No, no, I can't believe that. I won't allow this," Dr. Hayes insisted.

"It is true. Remember the night when Annie was a child, and she pulled you outside to see the angel?"

Dr. Hayes gasped, "How did you know about that?"

"Look at me Dr. Hayes. Do you remember me?" I trembled and hoped I was doing the right thing. If Dr. Hayes reacted badly, he may never allow me to see Annie again. If she lived, I would be watching her from the shadows once more banned from her life by her father. Even if the doctors and Annie's father didn't allow me to give her a transfusion, I will do it anyway. I will take her, go to the island, and I'll perform the transfusion myself if need be. I will save her with or without permission. Even if I have to steal her out from under their very noses, I will take her from this hospital and save her life. Time is of the essence though. If I have to take her from this hospital, I have to do it immediately. Plus, I need to round up sterile equipment to use for the procedure. That could take time.

I pressed her father, "You are a man of faith. Have faith that I have come here to insure Annie survives."

"No, no, I can't take that chance. I can't lose Annie. I lost her mother, and I can't lose her too."

"Dr. Hayes, Annie is dying. I am the only one who can save her. Believe me, please."

"No, no, I can't," he sobbed.

I took Annie's dad's arm and gently pulled him into an empty stairwell down the hall from Annie's room. I began unbuttoning my shirt.

"What are you doing?" Dr. Hayes murmured clearly shaken when he saw the sheaths of my swords appear.

"I am doing what I must to convince you." A hint of a smile touched my lips. "Don't be afraid. I need to show you something."

"Who are you?" He looked as if he was ready to bolt through the door. Cautiously, I moved in front of the door to block his exit because I knew what I was about to do would scare him. I pulled my shirt from my chest and laid it over the stair rail. Unbuckling my pants, I let them fall and stood before Dr. Hayes in a pair of silver boxer shorts.

"This is who I am, a Nephilim, an Annunaki, the last of the race between the fallen angels and human women." With that, I lifted my chin and snapped my wings into place. I began to transform and grow toward my full stature as much as the open stairwell would allow me.

Dr. Hayes stumbled backward clamping a hand over his mouth, stifling the scream that hung in his throat. Before him, I slowly transformed. My head elongated, my bones cracked and popped and extended several feet, my feet grew until they almost touched the tip of his shoes, and he jumped as they moved toward him. Muscles plumped up as though being inflated by a pump with the material of my clothes first straining then ripping at the unrelenting onslaught of flesh, blood, and bone. I transformed into an immense, frightening, giant warrior. Towering feet above him, I snapped my alabaster Annunaki face in his direction. Shrinking back from my icy stare, he remembered me then. He remembered that night; the night he could never forget. The angel he saw in his yard years ago and I were the same. I appeared to be the same age now as then, and that knowledge frightened him. Annie was only a child then. She had aged, but I had not. Yet, there was the same face of chiseled stone that he remembered. Every feature the same: silver eyes turned dark, hair so golden that it seemed to glow, light seeming to emanate from my pores, and wings. The wings were unlike anything he had ever seen. Beautiful arched wings sprang from my back and filled the stairwell. I crossed my arms and drew out a sword in each hand with a hypnotic metallic sound finishing the memory for him.

"It is you," Annie's shaking father backed into the metal rail in the stairwell and whispered raising his eyebrows.

"I am Annie's protector. Annie has an incredible future in front of her. Because of this, there are evil things in this world that are trying to kill her. One of those evil things attacked her tonight. This is the reason I have come into her life. My sole purpose is to ensure that she lives."

"Are you a guardian angel?"

"No, I am a dark angel, but many thousands of years ago, I had a vision of Annie. I made a decision at that moment that I would not let these evil ones have her. I am committed to save her from the dark creatures that hunt her. I have the permission of Heaven to be her protector."

Just as quickly as I had transformed, I changed back. Shrinking back to my usual six feet, four inch height, I placed my swords back in their sheaths, picked up my shirt, and slid it back over my broad shoulders and swords. I apologized to Dr. Hayes for disrobing as I buttoned my shirt and buckled my pants. Annie's father swayed, and I was fearful that he may fall at my feet in a dead faint.

"It was necessary to lose the pants and shirts before I shape-shifted. I don't have a change of clothes. They would be in shreds now if I had not," I explained. I threw my shoulders back and up hoping to look formidable. "Please allow me to be a blood donor for Annie. My blood is eternal. It will heal her. Have faith in me for Annie's sake. If we could ask her, she would agree with me. She trusts me. If you don't give me permission, know this, I will do it anyway. I respect you sir, and I want your permission to save Annie. However, I will save her with or without your permission or the doctor's."

Dr. Hayes nodded mutely unable to speak. He swayed a bit again, and I took his arm and led him back down the hall to where to crowd of doctors and nurses waited in Annie's room.

Annie's Dad looked at her, then to me, then at each of the doctors crowding the room.

"Are you absolutely one hundred percent sure that she will survive the transfusion, Zell?" Dr. Hayes asked.

"I'm one hundred and ten percent sure," I answered. "Please Dr. Hayes allow me to do this for Annie."

Annie's father turned to Dr. Patel. "Do the transfusion,"

"We can't be held responsible for her death, and she will die yet again. This time she will be too weak for us to bring her back," Dr. Patel argued angrily, visibly shaken.

"Then get me a paper to sign releasing you from liability and the hospital," Dr. Hayes shouted. "And do it now!" Dr. Hayes too transformed from his meek and mild demeanor into a father not to be reckoned with.

Dr. Patel's face showed that he wanted to argue, but he didn't know what to say. All the other doctors were looking at Dr. Patel waiting for his decision.

"I'll get the release from liability form for you to sign. However, let me go on record and in front of all these witnesses by saying that I am totally against this, and Annie's death is on your shoulders," Dr. Patel stressed.

"I'm fine with that because my daughter is dead already if I don't try the transfusion. Correct?"

"Yes, she is not responding to our antibiotic therapy. A transfusion is her only chance," Dr. Patel acknowledged. "I'll have the nurse come get both parties and prep them." Dr. Patel left the room with the other doctors filing out behind him whispering and shaking their heads.

As soon as the entourage of physicians left the room, I crossed over and laid my hand on Annie's father's shoulder. He covered my hand with his own.

"I promise you sir that Annie will live," I stated solemnly.

"God help me. I only agreed because I fear it's the only hope Annie or we have," Annie's father sighed, his shoulders drooped, the fight in him fleeing quickly now. Within five minutes, two nurses entered the room rolling two tables on which to transport us to the emergency room.

"Dr. Patel wants the procedure done in an operating room in case he has to intervene," one of the nurses, Ms. Wittman, according to the badge clipped to her collar, told Dr. Hayes. Dr. Hayes nodded, and the nurse and two orderlies moved Annie to the table.

"Now you," the other tired-looking middle-aged nurse spoke to me.

"I insist on walking." The nurses and orderlies looked at me taking in my size and the set of my jaw, and they decided not to push the issue. Nurse Wittman, evidently the head nurse, looked at the two orderlies and nodded. One orderly rolled Annie out of the room, and the other rolled the empty table out of the room behind them.

"I'll have Annie back to you in no time," I said smiling warmly at Dr. Hayes.

"I'm counting on it, son," Dr. Hayes replied softly. In an unexpected move, Dr. Hayes crossed the room and embraced me. I was so overcome with emotion that I could not speak and swallowed hard to keep from sobbing. I never had a real father, and his emotional embrace touched me. I was beginning to love Dr. Hayes just as I loved his daughter.

"I won't let you down, sir," I remarked and strode quickly from the room following the nurse and orderlies.

The nurse turned and stopped me at the door of the operating room and handed me a hospital gown.

"I don't need to wear that just for someone to stick a needle in my arm," I said refusing to take the gown. I was concerned that I would have to leave my swords if I undressed.

"I'll have to authorize this through Dr. Patel. Wait here." With that said, she turned and entered the operating room. Within minutes, she returned.

"Dr. Patel says to slip on the gown over your street clothes, and take your shoes off and wear these blue sterile slippers. We just need a sterile environment," the nurse explained almost apologetically opening a door to a little dressing room when she finished.

"Certainly," I replied and moved into the small room and shut the door. The room was more like a small closet with a bench on one wall. It was so narrow that my shoulders touched the parallel walls. I took off my shoes and slipped on the blue cloth slippers. Then, I checked my swords to make sure they were securely in place. The swords would be exposed in a backless hospital gown. I could not be sure that a dark being would not try to attack again while Annie was vulnerable. I slipped on the gown over my clothes. Stepping back out into the hall, I saw Nurse Wittman waiting on me.

"Sorry, I forgot to give you this. It's a shame to cover that gorgeous head of hair but . . ."

"I know–a sterile environment," I interrupted pulling a blue cap made of the same blue gauzy material as the slippers over my hair.

"Follow me," she ordered in a no-nonsense manner.

The cold air in the operating room hit me taking my breath and making me glad that I had not undressed. I would be freezing now if I had. I was not a fan of cold weather. I've been around long before heating units were invented. I've lived in incredibly cold climates. I remember when I used to keep warm by wearing layers of hides and sitting by a fire. There is a lot wrong with the modern world, but central heat and air are an amazing invention. I sometimes yearn for the simple life of yesteryear but never on a cold winter's morning.

Annie lay on an operating table moaning next to my empty one. I moved quickly toward her and was sitting on the table next to her in a flash.

Nurse Wittman tied an extra-long rubber hose around my arm just above my elbow. Evidently, the blood technician had already spread the word.

"Wow," she commented, laughing a bit as she glanced at the tired-looking nurse standing alongside her pointing to my huge biceps.

I smiled at her and winked at the other nurse who smiled back at me making her look years younger. They giggled like school girls. Nurse Wittman gave me a rubber ball to squeeze while she searched for an appropriate vein. On the fourth squeeze, the ball burst with a pop causing both nurses to jump. They fell into gales of laughter causing a stern look from Dr. Patel, who just walked into the room.

"Eh, never seen that happen before in my twenty-three years of nursing," the now not-so-tired looking nurse giggled.

My eyes shone mischievously, and both nurses sighed. As Annie would say, "The Zell Starr Fan Club just increased by two."

"Are you sure you want to kill this girl," Doctor Patel asked as he slid the needle into my vein.

"I would never hurt Annie. I know this will save her. Please trust me."

Dr. Patel grimaced in silence and began the procedure.

"You know this is extremely rare. We just don't do transfusions from person to person anymore. Everything goes and comes from a blood bank after the blood has been tested multiple times."

"In this case, a blood bank doesn't help Annie," I argued.

"That is the only reason I am allowing this madness," Dr. Patel answered, turning to look as several of the doctors that were in Annie's room filed into the operating room in scrubs, "but I want you to know this girl has a zero percent chance of recovery. I also want you to know that either way she is going to die. She will not live long enough for us to get a donor's blood to her, and you're going to kill her with your blood. Either way, she has a zero percent chance of surviving this day."

"Doctor," Nurse Wittman called to Dr. Patel. "The patient's temperature is 107 degrees, and her blood pressure is dropping fast."

Doctor Patel moved to Annie's side and began checking her vital signs himself. "This is not good," he murmured. "She may not live long enough to complete the transfusion." The other doctors in the room moved to check the monitors too. Everyone seemed to hold their breath as an unconscious Annie panted and groaned.

Doctor Patel walked back to my side. He leaned over and spoke quietly to me. "The average patient needs a transfusion of three and one-half pints of blood. The usual donation of blood taken from a donor is two pints. This could be dangerous for you if we take more than two pints."

"I signed the release of liability too. I will be fine. Give Annie what she needs—everything she needs. Even if it means my life is put in jeopardy, Annie must survive," I said emphatically. The doctor nervously patted my arm and returned to Annie's bedside. Long minutes stretched into an hour as the first pint disappeared into Annie's body and a second pint began. When the third pint began, Dr. Patel checked my vital signs to see how I was enduring the transfusion. He was surprised that my vital signs were not only normal, but they were in the excellent range.

Annie seemed to be resting easier, but her temperature still raged. When at last the transfusion was complete, Dr. Patel moved her to the intensive care unit. I was moved to a recovery room, but I was on my feet within minutes. Nurse Wittman stopped me at the door.

"Dr. Patel has ordered that you stay in the recovery room for at least an hour," she said sternly.

"I must go to Annie."

"She is in the intensive care ward. They will not let you in."

"I'll sit by the door."

"She has the best care that this hospital can give where she is," Nurse Wittman argued.

"You don't understand. I know she is going to get well, but she is in danger from another source. Something hunts her," I lowered my voice as I pleaded. I had a feeling I could take her into my confidence.

"Something hunts her?" Nurse Wittman echoed puzzled, and her eyes grew wide.

I ignored her question. "I have signed a release of liability, so I should be free to go." I argued. "Please, Annie is in danger, and it is not from a disease. My blood will heal her. Something stalks her."

Nurse Wittman's eyebrows raised, and again, she repeated my words. "Something stalks her?"

"I can't tell you any more than that," I sighed, "but I am her protector." Sternly, I met her gaze.

Nurse Wittman drew back as her gaze traveled to the tanned face of the young man before her. Her heart wrenched a bit at the anguish in it. Then, she let her gaze travel down to the bulging biceps of his arms and the muscled chest that not even his loose shirt could hide. Her mind wandered thinking that he was worthy to be on the cover of GQ magazine. He was impeccably dressed now that he had lost the hospital gown. He stood there silent and strong waiting for her approval, and she thought that he could very well be Annie's bodyguard. Maybe he was telling the truth. No, she was sure he was telling the truth. She didn't know how she knew, but she knew. She thought there was something spiritual about him. Somehow, she didn't think he would lie about this. She made a decision.

"OK, but I'll be down in thirty minutes to check your vitals. You had better be sitting in the waiting room in the Intensive Care Ward. I could lose my job," Nurse Wittman plainly stated.

"I'm not leaving this hospital until Annie leaves," I assured her.

"I wish someone was as devoted to me as you are to your Annie," she sighed.

"Thank you," I smiled and bent to kiss her lightly on the cheek. Nurse Wittman blushed.

"Go on with you then," Nurse Wittman shooed me away with a sweep of her hand.

I started walking down the hall, but I stopped and turned. "What I told you about Annie being in danger—could we keep that confidential?"

"Of course, no one would believe me anyway. Intensive Care is on the second floor."

I respectfully made a deep bow, and then I was gone. In the blink of an eye, I was gone. Nurse Wittman moved into the corridor and looked down it. I was no longer there.

"Humph, there *is* something different about that young man."

Thirty minutes later, Nurse Wittman found me sitting by the Intensive Care Ward door on a chair I borrowed from the waiting room. She checked my pulse, perfect. She checked my blood pressure, perfect. She checked my temperature, 98.6 degrees.

"Do you feel dizzy, nauseous, or weak?" She asked me.

"I feel well," I answered.

"You are well," she laughed. "Better than well, perfect. I am going back to my floor now where the sick people are located. If you feel dizzy, lightheaded or sick to your stomach, you have a nurse on this floor call me."

"I'll do that," I smiled at her, "and thank you."

⟋⟍3.Annie

A BLINDING LIGHT FLASHED. I BLINKED MY eyes and the light while still brilliantly bright did not hurt my eyes. I looked around me, and I seemed to be floating near the ceiling. Confused, I looked down. I could see Zell lying on a bed next to a girl on a separate bed. Doctors and nurses worked around Zell and the girl. I drew closer because I wanted to be near Zell. That is when I noticed that the girl next to Zell looked like me. I started to cry because in that instant I knew that I was dead.

"Don't cry sweetheart."

I stopped crying because the voice was so gentle. I was at peace and felt as though a great burden had been lifted from my shoulders. Instantly, I was in another place. I was standing knee deep in flowers in the most beautiful place you could imagine. A waterfall tumbled gently over rocks with amazing colors. Flowers grew in every inch of this place until they resembled a carpet. Willow-like trees blew gently in a soft breeze, and petals from the flowers that adorned them blew softly around me. Someone was walking toward me. I could tell it was a woman because of her long flowing hair and the gracefulness of her step. The flowers seemed to pass right through her as she walked instead of being trampled. And the colors—

the colors were brilliant and beautiful in shades and hues that did not exist on Earth.

"Annie." She held out her arms and called to me.

I took a step forward squinting. Her voice was familiar.

"Annie," she said again calmly. Her love enveloped us like a cloak.

"Mother!" I cried out jubilantly and ran for her. I threw my arms around her neck not wanting to ever let her go. "Oh Mommy, how I have missed you."

"I have never left you Annie."

"Yes, you did mother when I was five."

"Only the human shell of my body Annie. My spirit and love have always been with you. You just need to stand still, listen, and look for me. For I am with you always. You have blamed yourself for my death. You have blamed God. You must stop. My death had purpose, Annie. Someday, you will know. Someday, you will understand. The reasons for my death are not important now. What is important is your destiny—your work. You must be about your work."

"I don't know what my destiny is Mother."

"Zell will help you find your destiny. Trust him, Annie."

"I do. I mean—I didn't at first, but now I do. He has been wonderful to me."

"You must hurry, Annie."

"Hurry?" I asked.

"Yes, dear. Your time is at hand."

"What do you mean my time? I must be dead now, so how can I accomplish my destiny?"

"You must go back. It is not your time to die. You hold the fate of the world in your hands, Annie. You must be brave. You must fight the evil ones. You will refocus the world on beauty and righteousness. The world will follow you Annie, but you must hurry there is not much time. Listen to Zell. He will guide you to your destiny and protect you. He loves you so. I never would have believed anyone could love you as much as I, but he would go to the very pit of Hell itself for you. Be kind to him, Annie."

"I don't want to go back. I want to stay with you, Mother."

"You must my darling. You are my baby. You will always be my baby. I have loved you always, but you must go back. Even if you were allowed to stay, I can't be that selfish. You belong to the world, sweetheart. Your destiny is greater than the two of us. Give your dad a message from me. Tell your father that I love him, and that our love is eternal. Tell him I miss him, but I am never far from him. I see his life, and I am proud of the path he has chosen. Tell him I want to thank him for being such a wonderful father. Tell him not to grieve after me. We will be together once more never to be separated. As will we, my beloved, my Annie. Whenever you long for me, I will come to you if you have faith."

"I have no faith."

"You have more faith than you know. Search your heart. Open your eyes. If you believe Zell is who he says he is, then you know there is a plan and an order to this life, and there is a dazzling existence after this human body wears out. Have faith Annie." Mother began to fade, and I cried out to her.

"No, Mom don't go." I felt a tremendous pull, and I was being drawn away from my mother with amazing speed.

"Mother!" I screamed, but her image faded as I was whisked away through a dark tunnel as the brilliant light faded and darkness took over.

ᘓ᠕4.THE AWAKENING

I AWOKE IN INTENSIVE CARE THREE DAYS LATER. My father was sitting beside my bed.

"Dad, where am I?" I asked.

Dr. Hayes jumped to his feet. "Annie?'

"Who else?" I joked weakly.

"You have been in a coma for days. The doctors did not believe you would come out of it," my father said grabbing my hand squeezing.

"What happened to me?"

"Don't you remember?" questioned my father.

"No," I answered simply.

"Zell found you in the woods near Lake Lanier. You called him for help."

I wrinkled my brow in concentration. What happened to me? Had Zell kissed me again causing me to forget the event in the woods? Even as that thought crossed my mind, the memories started to seep back into my consciousness. The images of bouncing around in Jon's truck with my hands tied behind my back, the hunting and fishing cabin by the lake, escaping by canoe from Jon were seeping back in bits and pieces. All of it was coming into focus. The frantic call from Zell—and then—I didn't want to think about the rest. I remembered Jonny leaving me alone in the woods when the creature stalked us. I recalled the creature attacked me. If Zell had not pulled me from the monster's great mouth, I would be dead right now. My body gave an involuntary shudder. Then, I remembered the pain. The pain had been unbearable. The last thing I remembered was Zell with me in his arms and the pain.

For long moments, I lay there with my eyes squeezed closed, trying to forget the memory of that incredible pain.

"Annie, are you sick? Should I call the nurse?"

"No, I'm feeling better." I barely managed to get the words out. "Where is Zell?"

"He is sitting just outside the door. You're in Intensive Care. They will allow only one of us at a time to see you. Zell is not family, but I insisted that he be allowed to see you. Zell." My father's voice trailed off.

"Zell what?" I asked him.

"Zell saved your life twice," my father confided.

"Twice?" I replied, puzzled. "It was more like six times, probably more," I thought to myself.

"Yes, he pulled you away from some creature that attacked you in the woods and brought you here. You died in route to the hospital. Zell gave you CPR. Due to his intervention and getting you to the hospital quickly, the doctors were able to bring you back. The attack made you very sick. Dr. Patel said you would die if you didn't have a blood transfusion. Of course, you know how rare your blood type is. That presented a very dangerous problem. Finding a donor and getting blood for a transfusion before you died gave you a zero percent chance of living," Dad explained.

"Why didn't I die?" I asked him.

"Zell," he stated flatly.

"Zell has my blood type?"

"No, that is the peculiar thing. No one knows what blood type he has. His blood type is unknown. Let me tell you, it has caused quite a stir in this hospital. His blood contains unusual antigens. His blood seems to be a match for any blood type. He stood up to everyone, even me, to be allowed to give you the blood you needed to save your life."

"That sounds like him," I groaned moving joints that were stiffened from days in a hospital bed.

"Annie," Dad whispered conspiratorially leaning close to me. "Has Zell revealed any personal information about himself to you?"

"What are you talking about?" I frowned at the catch in my chest that was caused by his words. My father scanned my face. I had never been able to lie to him.

"We can discuss it later," he said and relaxed sitting back in his chair.

"I want to get out of here," I complained to my father.

"I'll talk to the nurse and see if she can get Dr. Patel to come in," he said getting up to find the nurse.

Dr. Patel walked in the room within fifteen minutes. He checked me out over and over again. Perplexed, he put his palm on his forehead, pushing back dark, thick hair. My dad was in the hall talking to Zell.

"I have never seen or even heard of a recovery like this. You should be dead now," Dr. Patel said, leaning over the bed talking in a low tone as if confiding a secret. "Your friend," Dr. Patel looked toward the hall in what looked to be mild fright. He never finished his sentence. He patted my hand and cleared his throat. "I'll have you moved out of intensive care, but I would like to keep you here for another twenty-four hours to make sure you do not have a set-back. However," he added, "it looks as though you have made a complete recovery." He looked to the door again with an expression on his face that I could not read. Was it worry, fright, or bewilderment? I wasn't sure. Slowly, he tore his gaze from the door and looked at me again. "I'll have the nurses rigorously check your vitals all night. I'll check you again in the morning. If everything looks good, I don't see why you can't go home then," he finished smiling weakly.

By the time I was moved out of Intensive Care, my eyes were drooping. I fought against the sleepiness that threatened to overtake me. I fought to keep my eyes open. I wanted to see him. I had to see him. I wanted to touch him. I wanted to know if Zell was my reality, or if he was a mixture of dreams and nightmares. As the door opened and I left the subdued light of Intensive Care into the glaring lights of the hospital corridor, I saw him, and my heart skipped a beat. Leaned against the wall at the end of the corridor, he was waiting. I was bedazzled by the beauty of him once again. His golden hair glowed as if it had a life of its own, silver eyes smiled at me from beneath long, dark lashes. Muscles strained against the material of his jeans on the leg that was propped against the wall. His signature untucked, button-up shirt, which hid the tools of his trade, fell loosely against his hands that were crammed into the pockets of his jeans. When he saw me, the light that came into his silver eyes made me even weaker. I smiled faintly at him, and he returned it with a brilliant smile of his own. As the orderlies rolled my bed past him, I reached for his hand. Gently, he grasped it with his own, and he walked in silence beside me all the way to a private room in an adjoining corridor.

He stood and watched as I was moved from the mobile bed to a bigger, more comfortable hospital bed. After the hospital personnel left the room, he moved to the side of the bed taking my hand in his. He opened my hand and kissed my palm. Then he pressed my hand against his face closing his eyes. He moved my hand just over his eyes trying to conceal the emotion that lay within them, but I felt my palm go damp with his tears. Abruptly, he stood up turning his back to me and walked to the window where he gazed into the night. When he turned back to me, he was composed once again, and a brilliant smile lit his face though his eyes were still sad.

"I was afraid you were lost forever to me. I am so sorry Annie. I promise that I will never leave you alone again."

"That is a big promise," I sighed. He smiled, and I closed my eyes and slept.

Sun streaked through the hospital window warming my cheek. I opened my eyes and looked about the room. Zell sat in a chair reading a book.

"Hi," I greeted him.

He turned to me, and his solemn face broke into a smile. He closed the book with a snap and rose. Zell walked to the side of my bed, and he bent to place a warm kiss on my forehead.

"Your father has left you in my care while he went home to shower and change."

"I wonder when the doctor will be in. I want to go home." I had to exert extreme effort to keep the whine out of my voice.

"It shouldn't be long now," he answered stroking my arm.

"May I talk to you about something?" I asked Zell.

"Of course," he answered moving a chair to my bedside, so he could sit and talk.

"First of all, I want to thank you for saving my life once again and by doing so putting yourself in great jeopardy. I know that by exposing the fact your blood type is unknown, yet will co-exist with any blood type and actually has healing properties that you possibly have put yourself in great danger."

"You worry too much," Zell said quietly still stroking my arm.

"Zell, there is something else I want to tell you. I'm afraid you will think I'm crazy, but I had a vision of my mother," It took a moment for Zell to realize what I had just confided.

"Are you sure? When?"

"When I was having the blood transfusion, I seemed to just lift out of my body. I could see you on the table beside me, and the room—the room was crowded with doctors and nurses. Then my mother was standing next to me. The next thing I knew, we were in a beautiful place much like your island. My mother said that I must be about my work. I asked her what work she spoke of. She said that you would know what we must do. She said we must begin now. We must hurry before the world gives into the evil ones. She said that we will refocus the world on beauty and righteousness. Then, she held me and told me she loved me. Mother called me her baby, and she said that I would always be her baby. She told me not to hold anyone responsible for her death especially myself. Mother said that someday I would know the reason she was taken from me. She said that she would see me again, and she was adamant that it wasn't my time to die. I begged her not to go, but she simply said that she must. Mother gave me a message for my dad. She told me to tell Dad that love is eternal, and they will be together again. She told me to tell him how much she loves him. Finally, she said that I must return and left me. I would think it just a dream, but I could see everything that was going on. I saw my dad in the waiting room praying. I could tell you every word that the doctors and nurses uttered. It was real Zell."

Before Zell could comment, the door swung open and Dr. Patel entered the room. Without a word and with only a panicked look in Zell's direction, he placed the stethoscope on my chest and listened to my heart. Then he shined a small light into my eyes. Flipping through my chart, he paused on the last entries, and then he closed the chart with a snap.

"Your recovery is amazing. I see no reason why we should keep you here unless you have fallen in love with our cafeteria food."

"I think I can manage without it," I giggled suddenly lightheaded and happy with the prospect of going home.

"Give us about thirty minutes to get your paperwork in order, and you can go." He walked around the end of the bed to where Zell was now standing and held out his hand. "Thank you," he said simply. "I don't know how you did it, but you saved her life." With that, Dr. Patel turned and walked out of the room.

"Will you call Dad and tell him?" I asked Zell.

A smile was his only answer as he pulled his cell phone out of his pocket.

Within the hour, Dad had returned to the hospital, signed some papers, and took me home. Zell left his car at the hospital and rode home in the back seat of Dad's sedan.

Zell carried me in the house and laid me gently on the sofa. My father brought a pillow and blanket to make me more comfortable. Zell sat on the floor next to me.

"I'll be in the kitchen if you need me," Dr. Hayes told us.

"What day is it?" I asked Zell.

"It's Friday. You have been in the hospital most of the week," he informed me.

"On Monday our district basketball tournament begins."

"Are you sure that you will feel up to playing?"

"I'm not telling anyone, except you, of course, but I feel great. However, I'm going to milk this getting waited on hand and foot for all it's worth," I laughed whispering conspiratorially. "Also, I have a question." I looked seriously at Zell.

"Yes," he replied.

"Am I eternal now, too?" I asked my heart beating wildly in my chest waiting for his answer.

"I'm not sure," Zell replied, staring at my hand which he was holding. "All I'm sure of is that my blood runs through your veins now."

"I feel different. I feel strong and invincible." I teased pumping up my bicep.

"Maybe that feeling is euphoric and temporary after all that you have been through. Maybe, it is permanent. I don't know. Just don't you do anything crazy like step out in front of a bus to test it."

I picked up the remote and flicked on the television. "How about watching a horror movie?" I asked.

"You're out of control," Zell laughed shaking his head.

⎰5.LITTLE HELP

SCHOOL ON MONDAY WAS TORTUOUS. ALMOST everyone in school stopped me at one time or another to get the 411 on what happened to me. Jon was not at school, nor had he been since the kidnapping, and I left him out of the story that I related. I tried to make light of the situation. I was out canoeing. I stopped on the bank to rest. An unknown animal attacked me. Infection sets in. Blah, blah, blah. I thought the questions and the school day would never end.

Basketball practice was light since the first game of the district tournament was tonight at the Gwinnett County Convention Center. We only practiced for an hour. Then we were released to get dinner and to the game by our seven o'clock meeting time. Ours was the final game of the night. We played a crosstown rival, Gwinnett High School. Of course, Zell sat in the stands watching and waiting for me to finish practicing.

Zell and I drove through the McDonald's on the way to the game. Dad had a meeting at church and would not be able to make the game. As Zell drove and I munched on crispy fries, I reflected over the subtle change in the relationship between Dad and Zell. Dad had liked Zell before, but since the attack, he trusted him completely with me. I know Dad was grateful to Zell for the transfusion that saved my life, but even that did not account for the way my dad looked at Zell. I wondered if something had transpired between them while I was ill, but neither would talk much about the days when I had lingered somewhere between life and death.

When we arrived at the Convention Center, Matthew and Christopher were sitting on the tailgate of Matthew's truck killing time.

"No need to hurry," Christopher yelled across several parked cars to us, "the games are running behind."

"Okay, thanks," I yelled back. Zell threw up his hand in greeting. Matthew and Christopher both jerked their heads nodding a greeting to Zell. Even though Zell was incredibly handsome and some of the boys had been jealous of him at first, practically all the guys, aside from Jon, liked and respected him now. Perhaps the reason they accepted him was because Zell was very clear that I was the object of his attention and affection. While he treated the other girls at school in a friendly, respectful manner, he never responded to their flirting with him. In other words, their girlfriends were safe around Zell. Even if girls flirted madly with him, their flirting was not reciprocated but discouraged. It had not taken the rest of the female population at Mill Creek High School very long to figure out that while Zell was available, even in the first days when I was still considered Jonny's girlfriend, he did not see them as girlfriend material much to their chagrin. Zell was a gorgeous guy who cared about me. I would never have to worry about him flirting or going out with other girls behind my back. Those facts were immensely comforting. Perhaps it was a moot point, but maybe I should go steady with Zell. I know he already asked Dad if he could court me, but I totally rejected and ignored that whole concept up until now. I mean, everyone already accepted that we were a couple, right? I thought about it, but yet, I felt like I was giving in. I felt as though I would be giving up my dreams.

Zell interrupted my train of thought. "Annie, do you know what I have dreamed of and waited on for six thousand years?" Zell asked, leaning close, only centimeters from my lips, passion clouding those beautiful silver eyes of his.

"What?" I asked. Trembling, I was sure that he spoke of me.

"Something so incredibly tempting and desirable?" His sweet breath filled my nostrils making me weak.

"What?" I asked again leaning toward him breathing heavily.

"Something that is the love of my life, and I never want to live without again?" He asked, brushing his lips against mine.

"No, tell me," I whispered, feeling as if I was melting where I sat.

"A Big Mac, fries, and sixteen ounce cola," he announced sitting back and taking a big bite of his burger.

"All this time, I thought you were a nice guy!" I huffed.

"What sweetheart? Did you think I was speaking of you?" He asked with a devilish grin.

"I'll tell my dad that we're no longer courting because I was dumped for a Big Mac." We both laughed until I choked on a piece of a French fry that I had not swallowed.

We finished our meal sitting in his Lamborghini with Zell telling me some of the humorous stories of his past. He told me of the time he agreed to perform in one of Shakespeare's plays only to arrive in the dressing room and be dressed as a woman. A woman who towered over all the other actors. He reminded me that in Shakespeare's day male and female parts were both played by male actors. But he, being the big, brawny type, never thought Shakespeare would cast him in a female role. Zell said that when another actor tried to kiss him that he had pulled a dagger and put it to the actor's throat. The actor whined that the kiss was in the script, and Shakespeare fell out in the floor laughing at the consternation of both actors.

We were having so much fun that I regretted the fact it was time to meet my team. I got out of Zell's car and reached for my gym bag. Zell reached over me and beat me to the bag and picked up another silver colored bag.

"What's that? I asked, referring to the bag he was holding.

"An emergency kit. Just in case . . . ." He trailed off. He needn't explain further. I understood. Zell walked me to the dressing room, and he brushed my cheek with his lips.

"I'll be close by if you need me," he whispered.

Kate took me by the arm and pulled me into the locker room.

"Looks like you two are getting sear-e-ous," she gushed.

"I like him," I murmured shrugging my shoulders.

"I think you two are in l - o - v - e," she spelled out laughing. "

"He is fun and kind of cute."

"Kind of cute?" Kate's mouth dropped open in shock.

"He should be on the cover of People Magazine as the sexiest man in the world. Move over Channing Tatum and Bradley Cooper."

Coach Neely called the team together before I could comment on Kate's statement, but I blushed and silently agreed whole-heartedly. He went over the starting line-up and assigned me to guard one-on-one a potentially deadly, three-point shooting, point guard on the Gwinnett High School's team.

The game was exciting with the lead teetering back and forth between us and Gwinnett. Kate scored three pointer after three pointer. She was hot, but she was as equally cocky as she was hot tonight.

"I'm available for autographs after the game," she leaned over and whispered to the Gwinnett guard who was assigned to keep her from hitting those three point shots. Neither team was ever more than three or four points out in the lead. I had held their best shooter to only four buckets, but it was exhausting work. In the middle of the third quarter, Kate scored a three point shot bringing us once again in the lead, 89-88. When the roar of the crowd settled down after Kate's basket, I could hear screams just beyond the double doors leading into the gym from the lobby. I looked to the stands where Zell sat with Matthew and Christopher and locked eyes with Zell. With a thundering boom, the double doors which connected to the lobby crashed open and standing in the open doorway, filling it with his size, was the creature from the woods. The creature stood on his hind feet and roared. In the blink of an eye, Zell was standing in front of me. People in the stands rose to their feet in horror, screaming and jumping from the bleachers. Dozens of frightened people stampeded past me on the court for the doors at the opposite end of the gymnasium. My gaze swung back to the creature as he moved on to the court. Half-standing, half-crouching the great beast lifted its wrinkled, blackened snout to sniff the air. Long black hair covered its body with the black fading to a silver color around its snout and eyes. Long, pointed ears covered in black and silver hair stood twitching on his great head. A mass of teeth crowded his enormous mouth, and I wondered how this beast could possibly close his great snout. Red eyes that seemed to be mere slits flitted first in one direction and then another. Bloody saliva dripped from the pointed ends of rows of fangs. It appeared to be an animal, but the creature had joints that made its legs resemble more human-like appendages. The ends of its legs were shaped more like a hand than a paw. Long, slender finger-like digits curled under slightly with four to five inch deadly nails. The gym scene was pure bedlam. A police officer entered the gym from the doors at the opposite end of the gym with his revolver drawn and pointed at the beast.

Everything blurred. Ghostly forms ran by me as the stands emptied. Standing still, a ringing in my ears replaced the screams of the beast and the spectators as they fled. I stood transfixed by the spectacle around me. Blood started exorbitantly pumping, pounding, and drumming in my ears. I didn't think these things wanted to be seen in public. I thought their modus operandi was to attack under cover of darkness when I was alone. My vision narrowed so that I seemed to have tunnel vision. All I could see was that dark Everest across the gym roaring and screaming.

Two more police officers ran through the double doors at the opposite end of the gym from the creature.

"Run, Run to your cars!" One officer shouted at the frenzied crowd. He could not fire through crowds of people as he tried to advance toward the creature. Waves of the fleeing mob hit him, pushing him back each time he made a little progress in the direction of the creature. The other officer still stood just inside the door weapon drawn. His hand that held his revolver shook so visibly that I could see it from where I stood at midcourt. A tsunami of people surged against the gym doors making it impossible for anyone to leave. An island of people formed around the doors screaming and clawing to get out.

"We have to go," Zell called to me grabbing my arm and attempting to move in the direction of the escaping crowd.

"No, I won't leave until everyone is safely out," I tried to tell him over the noise of the retreating crowd. "I'm the reason it's here. I don't wish for anyone to get hurt because of me. I don't want that thing chasing me through crowds of innocent people."

"We have to go. I can't change in front of all these people. My identity will no longer be a secret."

"Then hide under the bleachers, or go somewhere and change."

With a sigh of exasperation, Zell dragged me toward the bleachers pausing long enough to grab the silver bag that lay two rows behind our team seats.

"Don't move," he ordered as he ducked behind the bleachers. I looked to where the great beast had cornered a teenage girl with blond hair who resembled me very much. Oh God, did that beast mistake her for me? His head lowered and instantly I was in the parking lot outside the gym standing alone in the blackness of the night confronted by a similar creature. Growling and snarling, the great beast's head lowered preparing to pounce. Memories of another night not too long ago kept me rooted in place. Mixed with reality, flashes of previous attacks intertwined so that I was unsure of what was going on around me. The menagerie of scenes shifted back to the cornered, defenseless girl, and I knew he was getting ready to kill her. I shook my head to clear my thoughts. No, I can't let this girl die because this beast hunts me. I tore myself from the trancelike state that I had fallen into when Zell left my side. Ignoring Zell's order to stay put, I began to run across the floor of the gym yelling at the beast.

"Hey, here I am," I screamed, shouting and waving my arms. "I'm the one you want." The beast turned to face me forgetting the girl, and she slipped into the surging tide of people. Matthew and Christopher ran to my side.

"What are you doing?" Christopher shouted at me.

"I couldn't let him kill her," I cried out my chest heaving as if I had just run a marathon.

"Get ready because he's coming to kill you now. Where is Zell?" Matthew asked, attempting to raise his voice over the screams from the crowd.

"I've lost him," I replied with a shaking voice.

"Would you look at that?" Christopher exclaimed, staring transfixed toward the end of the bleachers where Zell had disappeared. Helplessly, I tore my gaze from where the creature stalked toward me glowering, and I followed Christopher's pointing hand.

There was Zell fully transformed. Gone were his clothes. Instead, he wore a chest plate of gold with huge silver medallions which connected golden plates of armor that covered his shoulders to the chest plate. On his forearms were silver and golden plates formed perfectly to fit. The protective plates ran from his elbows tapering to his wrists beautifully formed, etched, and carved. The chest plate ended in a V in front of his lower abdomen and a great silver belt circled his waist, followed the dip of the V, and changed to mail, a flexible armor of interlocking rings, flowing over muscular thighs to just above his knees. At his knees, delicate silver armor covered his knee caps followed by a single golden armor plate which ran down his shins to his ankles. Silver-colored boots began where the armor plate ended. More than his usual three sheaths hung from his broad shoulders, and he walked toward Matthew, Christopher, and me drawing two great swords from their sheaths as he walked.

Some of the people in the retreating crowd forgot their fear and stopped in their tracks to watch him. Several used their cell phones to snap photos and videotape him. Kate's dad, who had been filming the game, did not leave with the crowd but turned and filmed the great monster on the court. When he saw Zell coming across the court, he focused his camera on Zell. A couple of other parents who had cameras at the game to take pictures of their competing offspring stopped in flight and were snapping pictures of Zell.

The sight of him was unbelievable—dazzling even. Long golden hair flowed out behind him as he walked. His size was immense, eleven, twelve, or thirteen feet tall or taller, with muscles bulging from his naked thighs and biceps that peeked through his armor. His silver eyes turned black as cobalt set in a perfect, handsome face which at first glance seemed to be chiseled from stone. His wings . . . His wings were breathtaking. The height of the gymnasium ceiling allowed him to fully extend them. Beautiful, long white feathers with a silver and blackened rib outlined each wing as they reached out as if ready for flight. The end of each feather was tipped in silver, then black making a striking contrast to the stark white of the feathers. The soft glow that surrounded his wings and his hair made him look like a great, avenging angel. So massive was he, I was afraid he would hit his head on the powerful lights which hung suspended from the gymnasium ceiling. I had never seen him in full regalia such as this. He flipped both swords over and grabbed the tips of their blades. Zell extended the hilt of each one to Matthew and Christopher.

"Protect Annie until I return," he ordered. Matthew and Christopher, both offensive linemen on the Mill Creek football team, were muscular and massive in their own right. They howled in delight. They were always ready for a good rumble. Matthew moved to my right side, and Christopher moved to my left.

Zell began to walk away dropping the sheaths which belonged to Matthew and Christopher's swords at their feet. He stopped and turned to me withdrawing a long dagger from the wide silver belt. Bending close to my face, he whispered, "I made this for you." I looked at the beautifully engraved hilt of the dagger. My name, Annie, was engraved in a familiar, elegant handwriting. Diamond chips set in the silver of the hilt made it sparkle brilliantly. It was longer than the regular blade of a knife yet delicate and slender, but not the full length of a sword. Surprisingly light, I loved it immediately knowing Zell had made it just for me.

"This is so cool," Matthew crowed.

"Bring it on," Christopher yelled in the direction of the creature. The creature lifted its great head and let out a deafening roar as if in response. It paused momentarily, then crouched and began to race toward them. In return, Zell began to run toward the great beast. When the creature was within twenty feet of Zell, it gave a great leap into the air. Zell leaped from the floor to meet the creature midair. The collision made the floor of the gym shake and rumble. Many of the people, who stopped running from the monster when they saw Zell, fell to the floor from the quake that shook the gymnasium. The creature snapped his mighty jaws at Zell, who avoided the assault. Zell grabbed the hair on the monster's head and swung himself up on its back. The creature screeched and roared in protest. Zell drew one of his great swords and thrust it into the creature's neck. The creature reared up on its hind legs and then dropped and rolled over and over trying to dislodge Zell from his back. Zell lost his grip and rolled away from the creature. The great beast seized the opportunity to try to get to me. As it bounded toward me, Matthew and Christopher pushed me behind them and raised their swords. Zell leaped onto the beast's back once again grabbing the great mane of the creature. With all his might, he pulled the hair on the creature's head, causing the giant creature's head to whip backward. The creature twisted and reared up lifting its front legs from the floor.

"Sink your swords into its heart," Zell yelled to Matthew and Christopher from the back of the creature.

They did not hesitate. In unison, both boys thrust their swords into the chest of the creature. With great screams, the creature roared twisting and turning before dropping to the gym floor. Zell hung on and did not release his hold until the great beast crashed to the floor.

"Yeah man," Matthew and Christopher crowed giving each other a high five and jumping up to bump their chests together.

Zell jumped from the creature's back and drew out his flaming sword twirling it in the air until I was almost entranced by the swaying flames. Swiftly, he strode back toward the creature. Almost in the blink of an eye, he used the sword to separate the creature's head from its body. Then he withdrew his sword from the creature's neck. In like fashion, Matthew and Christopher withdrew the swords they had used to down the great monster. Zell then pierced the torso of the beast with his flaming sword, causing instant ignition of the body. He leaned over to pick up the head and tossed it at the feet of Matthew and Christopher.

"Keep the swords and the head for a souvenir gentlemen," Zell offered, "and thank you for your help." He turned to walk away, but stopped. Turning back to Matthew and Christopher, he raised the hilt of his sword to his face and bowed slightly giving them some sort of a salute. "Until we meet again," His wings stretched heavenward and then thrust down sending him zooming through the roof of the gym.

"Saweeet," Matthew and Christopher crowed.

The three of us, Matthew, Christopher, and I watched, heads tilted back, and mouths gaping open until he was out of sight, and then we turned and stood silently watching the beast burn. A police officer arrived with a fire extinguisher and put out the burning beast but not much remained.

"Who was that Matt?" Christopher exclaimed.

"Hey man, what was that?" Matthew shouted.

Matthew and Christopher turned the swords and sheaths over and over examining them and crooning with delight. They raised the hilts to their faces and bowed to each other imitating Zell's last action. When they began play fencing with one another that was enough, it was time to exit.

"See you at school tomorrow guys," I said turning to leave. On second thought, I stopped. I turned and embraced them both. "Chris, Matt, thank you for protecting me."

Both boys flushed with embarrassment and smiled.

Zell, dressed in his street clothes, came running through the doors into the gym calling to me.

"Are you okay, Annie?" Zell asked in a worried voice while the police officers continued to spray foam on the smoldering creature. Matthew and Christopher fought each other clinking and clanking with their newly acquired swords. "We were separated. I thought you were running for the car. I have been looking everywhere for you."

"You missed all the action," I chided, "Matthew and Christopher just saved my life." Both boys began to regale Zell with the story of their adventure.

"Who was this person that helped you, and where is he now?" Zell asked.

"He just flew off. Fought that thing like someone possessed, and then when it was dead, he was just gone." Christopher answered.

"Yep, he cut off the monster's head, threw it at our feet, and took off," Matthew agreed.

"I hate that I missed all the fun. Come on Annie. I'll take you home." Zell put his arm around me and pulled me toward the exit.

"Let's take its head to a taxidermist," Matthew yelled at Christopher.

"Saweeet!" Christopher yelled back.

"See you both tomorrow," Matthew called after us. Both of us waved goodbye to the two excited, young men.

"You made their day," I laughed.

"I think I made their year," Zell returned.

In the car, Zell exhaled deeply. "I assume that Matthew and Christopher didn't recognize me?"

"I think your secret identity is safe for now. You were pretty unrecognizable."

"Aside from the fact that you just finished battling a Dark One is something wrong?" I questioned.

"Something is very wrong." He only pushed back further in the seat staring ahead.

"What is it?" I asked, worried.

"A Dark One has never attacked in front of a crowd of witnesses before. Something strange is going on here," Zell mused as the sound of approaching sirens echoed in the dark night.

✑6.IN THE NEWS,AGAIN

EARLY THE NEXT MORNING BEFORE MY ALARM **even** went off, my cell phone rang. Kate's squeal pierced the cloud of fog that surrounded my still asleep brain.

"Turn on the television, quick."

Sleepily reaching for the remote of the rarely used television in my room, I pushed the power button.

"What channel?" I asked sleepily.

"Any of them. All of them," she squealed louder.

As the picture popped on the screen, I was there waving and shouting at the beast in the gym. The picture clearly showed the beast turning on me while the girl it had cornered escaped.

"It's all over every station. They are calling you a hero, or heroess, or whatever it is they call female heroes."

"Heroine," I added dryly, "and I'm not one." I took a deep breath as I saw Zell and the creature clash in midair. "Oh, wow!" The scene was impressive last night, but seeing it all replayed before my eyes dazzled me. It was all there too: Zell grabs the creature's neck and hoists himself on its back, thrusts his sword into its neck, pulls its massive head back, and Matthew and Christopher sink their swords into the chest of the monster. There, too, was Zell drawing his flaming sword and incinerating the beast while Matthew and Christopher ridiculously bumped chests and swatted high fives.

"Good Morning, America, has even picked up the video, and they are showing it over and over," Kate informed me.

"Where did they get this tape?" I asked her.

"When that warrior angel showed up, my dad didn't run like everyone else. He stayed behind and videotaped the whole thing. When we made it home, he showed it to me, and I put it on YouTube. I guess it became like an instant overnight sensation. It is kind of spectacular in a supernatural kind of way. They are saying on Good Morning America that there have been over a million hits on YouTube just in the past hour," Kate finished.

"Oh dear," I moaned. I didn't think Zell would be very pleased by all of this.

"You're going to be famous. Oprah will probably call you. Jimmy Fallon even," Kate swooned and rambled on and on about what famous personalities would most likely be in touch with me.

"I've got to go Kate. I'll see you at school." I hung up the phone and dropped back on the bed. I closed my eyes and sighed. I didn't want the attention or the onslaught of questions this tape was sure to invoke. Dragging myself out of the bed, I turned on the shower and let the hot water scald me. The burning sensation took my mind off the media frenzy that was sure to come. When I finished my shower, I wrapped my hair in a towel, threw on a bathrobe, and opened the bathroom door. There Zell stood in my room meticulously dressed in jeans and a soft gray shirt that set off his eyes perfectly.

"Don't you knock," I growled at him.

"Sorry. I was anxious to show you this. He opened the folded newspaper that he held in his hands. There in full color taking up most of the front page was Zell astride the creature driving his sword into the back of its neck.

"You're a dinosaur, Zell. What teen buys and actually reads a newspaper before going to school each morning. You need to start acting cooler."

"Dinosaur? Cool?" Zell looked at me puzzled.

"Yeah, stop buying newspapers. You are impersonating a teenager."

"But I check the stock market every morning."

"Duh, of course," I said rolling my eyes. The plight of the uber-wealthy was taxing; I'm sure. "Use your phone."

"My phone?"

"Yes, you have direct access on your IPhone." I snatched the paper out of his hands and sat down hard on the bed. Zell pulled out his phone and was scrutinizing it carefully.

"Really?"

"Really." I took his phone from him and downloaded the app.

"Thank you, Annie, but you need to look at the front page of the newspaper. This photograph disconcerts me somewhat," he explained. "In all the years that I have battled, first, the Annunaki, and then the Dark Ones, never has my picture been taken. Of course until the last hundred years, the technology was not there. Remember how I told you that I was always careful to lead others to the evil ones to keep my face and my name out of it?"

"Yes," I answered softly.

"I guess my identity is no longer secret," he sighed.

"But that is you in your Anak transformation; no one will link this to you. When you transform, you look different. You look so frightening that no one will ever know that it is you. Besides, the Anak is twelve feet tall or more even if someone did see the resemblance, how could they explain the size difference? Your secret identity is safe." I tried to reassure him laying a hand over his hand which held the paper. I even felt as though he and the Annunaki were two different people. Zell was so warm and kind, and the Anak was so cold and frightening.

"You were there. How long do you think it will take the detectives that handled the case at the Zoo to realize that you are the link?" He gazed worriedly into my eyes.

I saw his point. "It doesn't matter. If we have to escape to the island and live there, we will. If we have to go to the moon, we'll go . . . together. We are in this together," I reassured him.

He sighed, "I don't want you to go into hiding or have your life turned upside down because of me."

"My life," I began, "would be over already if not for you. I have to figure out a way to use this," I reflected deep in thought.

"Get dressed," Zell ordered. "I'll go back out and ring the doorbell."

"I didn't mean anything by the 'don't you knock' comment." I smiled at him realizing that Zell's concern was for me. He didn't want my life disrupted. I was his weakness. He could handle anything that came his way except for those things that disrupted my life. I tried to reassure him. "I'm fine as long as we are in this together."

"For your dad's peace of mind, I'll ring the doorbell." He smiled and hugged me to him for a moment, and then he moved to the door. He cracked the door open and looked into the hall. Turning to smile at me he said, "I'll see you in a moment." With that, he disappeared into the hall.

Quickly, I dried my hair. I had barely finished pulling on a pair of jeans and a silver top studded with rhinestones when the doorbell rang. Grabbing the silver jacket that matched it and a pair of silver sandals, I moved to answer the door. Thinking it was Zell, I opened the door only to have a big microphone shoved into my face.

"Can you comment on the events of last night, Miss Hayes," a female reporter shouted at me. Startled, my mouth dropped. I saw Zell drive up in his Black Hummer that he had decided to drive today instead of the Lamborghini.

"I have no comments. The video speaks for itself," I answered.

"The public deserves an interview Miss Hayes," the reporter snarled.

"I'll let you know," I said shakily shutting the door behind Zell as he came through it. I turned and walked to the kitchen with Zell at my heels. "Wow," I breathed sinking into a kitchen chair.

Dad came down the hall sleepily scratching his head. "What's all the commotion?" Zell and I shared a look.

"Something happened last night at the basketball tournament," I began.

Dad stopped in the hallway. "What?"

"Some kind of a gigantic animal came into the gym and started attacking people."

My dad's jaw went slack, and he pulled his glasses out of his pocket as if he couldn't comprehend what I was saying without his glasses on. I moved to the television in the living room and turned it on. There I was again shouting and waving my arms at the monster. I cringed when I saw the look on my dad's face. We all watched the television in silence. When the Anak came onto the screen, my dad's head slowly turned, and he looked warily at Zell.

"Oh my," he said, dragging out every vowel and consonant as he watched the Anak fight the creature. When the clip finished and the news announcer came back on the screen, Dad sunk into a chair. "Oh my," he repeated again.

"What do I do Dad? There are reporters outside."

Dad sat there for what seemed like an eternity. Finally, he spoke. "You put as positive a spin on this as you can, and you talk to them. I'm afraid they won't go away unless you do."

I knew he was right. I would have to talk to them, or they would continue to stalk me wherever I went.

"Okay," I sighed, "but I need a few minutes." Putting off the inevitable interview, I returned to my room and slowly sat down. For several minutes, I just sat there brooding over what I would say.

"Let them in," I said grimly when I returned to the living room. Dad opened the front door, stepped out on the porch, and closed the door behind him.

He returned several minutes later with five reporters, one for each of the local network stations, two national networks, and a like number of cameramen.

Jenny Harper, a perky brunette for the CBS affiliate station, was the first to speak.

"Miss Hayes, I know you must still be shaken from your incident last night, but can you tell the viewing audience why you stayed during the attack and did not run like most of the people at the scene?"

"I couldn't leave that young girl to the mercy of the creature without attempting to help her."

"Did you not have any concerns about putting yourself in jeopardy?"

"I really didn't think about me. I knew I had to try to help her. You see I believe that if good people stand by and do nothing, then evil flourishes; it wins. Besides, that thing was looking for me."

"What do you mean it was looking for you?" Ian McClung, a very cute, in a messy kind of way, Fox News reporter interjected.

"The Anak tells me that I have a destiny, and that is why these Dark Creatures hunt me."

"What is this destiny?"

"I don't know. It hasn't happened yet, but the Anak says that I will change the world. Don't get me wrong. I have a hard time believing that I will ever do anything to change the world. Evidently, these dark creatures believe that I have a destiny to undo their evil kingdom."

"Do you know this . . . this winged creature that came to your rescue?" Ms. Harper interjected.

"I have seen him before," I answered truthfully.

"Could you tell the TV audience about your first encounter with this winged giant?" Ian countered.

"I was leaving after a visit to the Atlanta Zoo. Several gang members surrounded me. They shot at me, and he just appeared and covered me with his wings. The bullets fell harmlessly to the ground." I looked at my dad from the corner of my eye, and I saw him go pale. I never told him about the trouble at the zoo. "Even after that, they kept coming for me. He saved my life by fighting them off."

The reporters were stunned into silence briefly looking at one another. Jessica Snyder, a CNN reporter was the first to recover.

"You mean you were the blonde girl who was involved in the murder of four people."

"I didn't murder anyone," I responded.

"Who did?" Ian McClung interjected.

"The same hero that saved us all last night, except it wasn't murder. It was self-defense. He saved my life. He gave them a chance to leave. They answered his request for them to leave by shooting at us." I tried to keep my voice even, yet it broke somewhat when I told them it wasn't murder.

"Is it true that you intervened and saved one of the thugs from dying at the hands of this winged creature?" Tina Davis, a tall, slim, raven-haired beauty from the local ABC affiliate station asked.

"Yes, that is true. It all happened so fast. But I wanted one to remain as a witness. I told him to go back and tell everyone that any evil from that point on will be met with swift justice, not from the law, but from an Avenging Angel. I told my attacker that obviously the . . . the . . .," I struggled for a word to describe Zell when he was standing right next to me listening, "warrior was not of this world. I told the guy to take a good look at him. If you ever commit an evil act again, he will hunt you down and find you. Your life is no longer your own. You must compensate for all the evil you have done. You must tell others that evil will be met with his sword. You must spend the remainder of your life helping those you have victimized, helping the helpless, telling of this night, and how your life was spared. I told him to run to the police and tell them his story. I told him that every word must be the truth, and he must live a good and decent life from that moment on or the angelic warrior, the Anak, would find him."

"Why do you call him an Anak?" Ian McClung piped in.

"That is who he told me he was. Actually, he belongs to the race of the Annunaki, the Nephilim, the race that was created between the fallen angels and human women. They were later called the Anak." I explained, shrugging my shoulder and raising an eyebrow.

"Is this Anak your own personal Guardian Angel?" Tina Davis queried.

"You could say that, but I believe he will protect any innocent not just me," I tried to explain.

"Isn't this Anak actually a cold-blooded murderer?" Jessica Snyder barked. I could feel Zell flinch beside me.

"No, he is not. I told you he gave them a chance to go, but they refused. They just kept coming, shooting at me, at us. They would not stop. He had no choice. They had guns, and he only had a sword to defend me. They would have killed me if he had not intervened. He will always be a hero to me, and last night, I would have died along with many others. Good people who didn't deserve to die would have been killed or injured if he had not come to our rescue."

"Why do you think that this Anak is here?" Ms. Harper retorted. "Why has he never been seen before?"

"I think the world is so full of evil that God has sent a special warrior here to protect us, and I believe he has been sent as a reminder that He has not forgotten us but loves us. I have to go to school now." I rose ending the interview. I couldn't believe that I just gave God credit for Zell. Yet somehow, I blurted it out.

Journalist Ian McClung jumped in front of me squeezing one more question in, "Is it true that you were mauled by a similar monster only a week or so ago?"

"Yes, it is," I answered quietly.

"Do you think this was the same beast that attacked you previously?" He pressed.

"I don't know. It was very dark the first time. I have to go now." Zell stood at the door with my school bag waiting. I kissed my dad and moved to join Zell with the cameras still rolling. I stopped at the door and turned to face the cameras and reporters once more. "He calls them the Dark Ones." I said. "The Anak called the beast a Dark

One." Zell opened the door, and we stepped outside into the slightly past dawn of a new day.

"You mean plural? Are you telling us there are others like this creature?"

"That's exactly what I am telling you." I turned to face him suddenly feeling strong and ready to fight these dark creatures wherever they found me.

Zell grabbed my hand, and we pushed through crowds of people to reach his vehicle.

"It's only 7 a.m. Where did all these people come from?" I asked Zell.

"You're news," he stated simply.

School was even worse. The parking lot was full of television vans, reporters, and camera crews. A reporter was interviewing Matthew and Christopher. I could tell by Matthew's and Christopher's body language that they were telling a whopper of a good story.

"Please pull into the back lot away from the cameras," I urged Zell. Whether it was luck or a brilliant plan, Zell did not drive the Lamborghini, and no one recognized us through the dark-tinted windows of the Hummer.

We crossed quickly through the back parking lot and slipped in the doors of the gymnasium without being noticed. Thankfully, Matthew and Christopher were keeping everyone entertained in the front of the school building with their retelling of the previous night's events.

We were early for school. A few people sat in the bleachers waiting, and we climbed a few rows up and away from everyone else and sat down.

"I feel sick," I said nervously.

"You handled the reporters brilliantly," Zell said, squeezing my hand.

"Do you really think so? I went ahead and told about the night at the zoo since you said it would be discovered anyway. I wanted to get a public explanation out there before the media got a hold of the information without one," I babbled on not giving Zell the opportunity to answer my question. "I'm worried about my dad. There was a lot of information that he knew nothing about. I saw the look on his face when I told of how the bad guys shot at us. I feel sick," I repeated. "If home had not been a madhouse, I wouldn't have come to school today."

"You can't run from your future, your destiny, Annie," Zell whispered.

"Is that what this is?" My voice trembled and my legs shook.

"You faced a great beast with such bravery, and you are frightened of a few human reporters?"

"But *they* are vicious," I laughed.

The day was a nightmare. The police arrived and moved the TV crews across the street from the school. Two detectives came and called me into an empty classroom to get a statement from me about the events surrounding the zoo incident. The news crews stayed and interviewed anyone who walked close enough for them to stick a microphone in their face. Everyone in school seemed to be on edge. No one said much to me all day. They just watched my every movement like something was going to happen.

Kate was the only person in school who seemed unaffected by the events of last night, and the presence of the media all around campus.

"Hey, Annie what's up?" Kate asked.

"Seriously?" I moaned.

"Everyone have their panties in a wad over the troll that showed up at the game last night?"

"Yes, news reporters were camped out in front of my house early this morning."

"Yeah, that freak ruined my shooting streak! I had Gwinnett shaking in their Nikes. I was hot as fish grease. I was hitting those threes and nuthin that Gwinnett guard could do about it."

"You're so humble, Kate," I giggled.

"Damn straight," Kate replied seriously.

The basketball tournament had been postponed for necessary repairs to the gymnasium. I followed Zell throughout the rest of the day hoping for invisibility. Finally, the day ended. Basketball practice had been cancelled, and Zell and I slipped out through the gymnasium to the back lot. We could not even drive down my street for all the cars, people, and news network's personnel parked in front of my house.

Zell dialed our home number.

"Dr. Hayes, this is Zell Starr. I attempted to bring Annie home, but we cannot get through without her being mobbed. I would like your permission to take her to my home." Zell listened.

"Yes, I will. You are welcome to come too." Once again, he listened.

"Yes, I will tell her. Thank you, sir," Zell pressed a button on the dash to disconnect the call. "Your father has given me permission to take you home with me. He wants to speak with you later. Kate was right. All the network talk shows have called for an interview plus Oprah, Monster Quest, Animal Planet, and the Discovery, Destination, Travel, and History Channels. He says their offers would be more than enough to pay your way through college and secure your future. Good Morning America wants you there in the morning. He said to take a couple of hours to think about it, and then give him a call.

"What should I do?" I asked Zell.

"I think you should go. Not because of the money. I can buy a college for you if you need a college fund, but because you need a platform. This is your destiny. This is why you were born. It is why I am here. What better platform than national television?"

"What should I tell them?"

"The same thing you told the local reporters." Zell finished as we pulled into the drive of his home.

"Do you mind if I sit by the lake for a while and think?" I asked him.

"Of course not. I'll go get us something cold to drink."

I sat down on one of Zell's comfortable lounge chairs and stared out over the sparkling, quiet lake. The gentle lapping of the water on the shore relaxed me. Zell was right. If I had the opportunity to be on national television and speak, that is what I needed to do. I just wanted to protect Zell though. I was so afraid of slipping and identifying him as the Anak. My head pounded with worry.

Zell brought out a pitcher of tea and two glasses filled with ice and some strawberry muffins. He filled the glasses with tea, handed me a glass, and sat down on the chair across from me.

"Cook loves the fact that I finally have friends. Every day she cooks something amazing just hoping someone will stop by. I believe she was rather bored of cooking just for me."

"I think I should tell your story," I explained to Zell biting into a muffin.

"My story?" He asked.

"Yes, it's much more interesting than mine," I said grimly. "Just think. A human and angel hybrid has a vision of a girl. He waits for thousands of years for her to be born. Then defends her from demons from hell. The tabloids would eat it up." I finished my glass of tea and pulled my phone from my pocket. "Please tell your cook thank you for me. These muffins are amazing." I punched in my father's cell number and waited for him to answer. "Dad, Zell said you needed to talk to me," I frowned as I listened to my dad. "Yes, I'll do it. Please make the arrangements, and Dad . . . Zell has to go too." I said after some hesitation.

Later that evening, we flew to New York City. I was scheduled to be on Good Morning America the next morning. Then, we were taking a flight to Chicago to be interviewed by Oprah. Finally, we were flying back to New York for appearances on the Today Show and The Early Show the following morning. The limousine that the Today Show sent for us arrived early, and we arrived at the station promptly at six a.m.

After the introduction and a video clip showing the television audience Monday Night's encounter with the Dark One, Ms. Roberts asked me my first question.

"Well, Annie, this has been quite a week for you. As I watch this video, I am intrigued that everyone else is running, and yet, you stand up to this creature that has this girl cornered. What were you thinking?"

"I'm not sure that I thought at all. I just knew that if I didn't help her, she would die. It's my fault that the Dark One was there at all. I couldn't have anyone hurt because of me."

"Why do you think this creature is after you?"

"I think that there is something that I will do with my life that threatens these creatures."

"Are there more than one creature?"

"Yes, many."

Is this the first time you have been attacked by a monster?"

"No, actually this is not the first time. I have been attacked several times," I answered.

"I never thought monsters existed, and now you tell me that you, a high school senior, has endured several attacks by these creatures?"

"I was the same. I didn't believe in anything that I couldn't see or put my hands on until recently. My mother died when I was five. I've been mad at God ever since. I've had to live almost my whole life without a mother. I ceased believing in anything. Then, this Dark One showed up and my defender, the Annunaki, saved me. It has been hard to remain skeptical about anything after meeting those two. The Anak tells me that I have a destiny. He says that I will do something to change the world. Look at me. I'm just an eighteen year old, average girl. I'm really not very brave at all. I find it extremely hard to believe that I will do anything to change the world. I have trouble deciding which pair of shoes to put on in the morning," I laughed nervously.

"What is this something that you will do that puts your life in such jeopardy?" Ms. Roberts asked, frowning.

"Honestly, I'm not sure yet. Maybe, it is that I am exposing and fighting back against a hidden darkness. Evil is so pervasive in our society today that everyone seems to take for granted. Perhaps, some people believe it is hopeless to fight against it," I explained. "I am here to tell the world that evil must be fought against, and we can and must win. We are not doomed to a future surrounded by murderers, thieves, and liars. If people are convinced that there is more to life than what is at the end of their fingertips, perhaps, that will encourage them to be a little kinder, more helpful, and to take a stand against evil wherever it may be found."

"Where do you think these creatures come from, and why haven't we seen them before?"

"The Dark Ones that is what Z . . ., the Anak calls them are Dark Angels. They come in many forms: vampires, werewolves, grotesque monsters, demons, or dark angels. I think they take on these forms just so that we will not recognize them for what they are. We will think them merely monsters, legends, the creatures of our nightmares. The evil creatures of our nightmares and folklore do exist. They are the Dark Ones. They all have one common thread though; they are Fallen Angels.

"Do you mean the Fallen Angels of the Bible?" Ms. Roberts gasped and raised her eyebrows.

"Yes, that is exactly what I mean."

"Why are they here, now?" She asked puzzled.

"They have always been here. I believe it is only lately they have been empowered to show themselves. I believe they are empowered because we tend to ignore the evil in our society today. We look the other way when evil presents itself."

"What do you propose that the average American do about it?"

"They are so many more good people than there are evil ones in this world. If every one of us stood together against evil every time it rears its dark head, we could defeat the Hitlers, the Stalins, the molesters, the muggers, the murderers, and the Dark Ones of this world. There is such apathy in the world today, especially in young people. I know. I am one. How many times do we allow bullies to terrorize fellow classmates, tolerate drug use among our friends, and stand silently by while others use filthy language and violate anyone they choose? How many people ran from that gymnasium? Only a handful stood up to the creature. Less than that will stand up for a fellow classmate that is being mistreated. There are Dark Ones among us that look just like you and I, and we allow them to victimize us and others. I, for one, will not tolerate this any longer. Albert Einstein said, 'The world will not be destroyed by those who do evil, but those who watch them without doing anything."

"Bravo. Annie, but let me get this straight. Are you telling me that the monsters of folklore actually exist?"

"I am telling you that the Dark Ones exist. They have enough power to take on or hide behind any evil form."

"Wow! I may not sleep very well tonight."

"Welcome to my world," I laughed.

"Annie, can you tell me about this Anak? The one who fights the monster in this video clip." She waited while the film clip was played again.

"I hesitate to talk about him, because what he has told me about himself will be hard for most people to believe even with the video evidence of him. I will tell you what he has told me. He is from the race of the giants, like Goliath, of Biblical times. Yet, he never succumbed to their evil ways. His father was a fallen angel and his mother, human. He has fought alongside good men against evil through the millenniums. If he exists and the Dark Ones exist, then there truly is a supernatural battle that rages on between good and evil. While that supernatural battle exists, there is also a natural battle against evil that needs to be fought. I think that's where I come in."

"He is extraordinary!" Ms. Roberts exclaimed watching a replay on the screen in the studio. "However, you are right in your assumption that all this is rather hard to believe. Do you really expect the American public to believe that there are Fallen Angels, Dark Ones, and a warrior called an Anak in this world?"

"I only ask them to believe their eyes. They can see the reality of this once hidden world for themselves. Dacula, Georgia, isn't Hollywood. This event happened, and it was caught on film. I know some will think that it was faked. Just research it. Come to Dacula. Interview those that were there. Matthew and Christopher, my friends who came to my aid, still have the head of this creature."

"Tell me more about this warrior which rescued you? Do you know anything else about him? Where did he come from?"

"There is only one Anak. He is the last of his kind, his race. He says that he had a vision of me when he was fourteen. He has waited for thousands of years for me to be born. He has made it his destiny to protect me."

"This is all so extraordinary that it is almost impossible to believe."

"Yes, I know, but you saw the video. They are probably hundreds of witnesses that can verify the attack of the Dark One. I am not claiming anything that cannot be backed up by evidence. I would probably not have believed any of this myself a couple of weeks ago. Now, I know these things exist."

"Could this be just a mutated wolf or bear that happened to . . ."

"Attack me several times in several different locations?" I interrupted. "That explanation is harder for me to believe than the explanation that I have just given you. Even if we could explain away the creature, how do we explain away the Anak?"

"Touché," Ms. Roberts answered. "Good luck to you, Annie and to your Warrior. We'll be following you, and we wish you all the best."

A network assistant rushed us from the studio to a waiting limousine. Dad, Zell and I rode in the limousine to a plane that Oprah had waiting for us at the airport.

"I'll be glad when all this is over, and we can go home," I moaned, leaning back into the plush seat of the plane.

"You're doing fine," Dad encouraged.

Zell was silent.

"Is something wrong?" I asked him.

"I think so," he replied.

"What?" I asked worriedly.

"That, I cannot answer. I just have a feeling of foreboding."

We all traveled the rest of the short flight to Chicago in silence.

From the time we landed in Chicago, everything was a whirlwind. We were rushed to a waiting limousine, and then to the studio. Upon arrival, Dad and I were taken to make-up. Zell refused to go on stage and was shown to a private room where he could wait. The tension increased as it drew closer to show time.

Oprah's assistant came to get Dad and me, and we waited just off-camera. Then I heard her, "My next guest has had a most amazing experience. In case you have been living under a rock somewhere and missed this video, we are going to show a few minutes of this unbelievable film."

For the next few minutes, Kate's dad's homemade film played. There must have been a few rock dwellers out there because I heard gasps of astonishment when first the beast showed itself, and when Zell walked into the view of the camera, the audience gasped in unison as if in one breath. When the film finished playing, Oprah's assistant ushered us on the stage. We walked over to where Oprah was sitting.

"Our next guest is Annie, the girl who stood up to the creature in the film. How are you dealing with all that has happened to you?" Oprah began.

"I take it one day at a time; in addition, I have a great support system: my father, my friends, and the warrior."

"Let's talk for a moment about him—this warrior. I and I'm sure the rest of the world finds him as intriguing as I do. Who is he and where did he come from? Never have creatures like these been filmed before."

"It's quite a long, incredible story, but he says he had a vision of me when he was fourteen, six thousand years ago. He has waited all this time for me to be born in order to protect me from the Dark Ones."

"And the Dark Ones being the creatures such as the one that attacked you a few nights ago?" She asked.

"Yes." I answered.

"You use Ones in the plural sense, so there are others?"

"I believe so. That is the second one of that type of creature that you just saw that has attacked me. I have also been attacked by other creatures."

"Such as?"

"At a cookout, I was attacked by a dark creature with fangs like a vampire. While the warrior was fighting it, I stabbed it through the back and heart with an umbrella pole. The Anak, then incinerated it. He always carries three swords with him. Two swords are crisscrossed against his chest, and the third he carries against his back. It is a flaming sword. He always separates the head from the body, and then he ignites the body with the flaming sword. He states it is the only way to kill them."

"Have there been other creatures to attack you?"

"At school a creature attacked when I was taking a short cut to the gym. It looked like an old wrinkled man with the face of a gargoyle, giant bat-like wings, and rows and rows of teeth that couldn't be contained within its mouth. The Annunaki, the warrior, he showed up at the last second and killed it."

"What is an Annunaki? I know it is this warrior on the film, but who is he?"

"He is from the race of the giants such as those in biblical times like in the story of David and Goliath. His mother was human and his father is a fallen angel."

"So you are telling me this myth from the Old Testament is real?"

"That is precisely what I am telling you."

"This is an incredible story. Do you think others have been attacked by these creatures?"

"It's quite possible that they have and not lived to tell about it as I have."

"Why are they coming for you?"

"They are evil. By exposing them, I am exposing evil to the world. We have to stop turning and looking the other way when natural and even supernatural evil presents itself. We have to fight against it. We should not stand by and wait for others to fight the battle for us. There are so few of them and so many good people in the world. All you have to do is have the courage and take the time to fight them. They count on our disinterest, on our disbelief. I'm not talking about supernatural evil here; The Anak will deal with the supernatural. I'm talking about the evil we see all around us: gangs, drug dealers, and murderers. Why do a handful of gang members and drug dealers terrorize a city?" I believe it is because we allow them to have power over us. We don't expose them. We don't report them. Why do parents allow drug deals to go down in schools? Why don't we take our schools back? Why do they allow children to be disrespectful and curse teachers? Why don't hundreds of parents show up at school every day until schools are the safe places they should be?"

The sound of lone someone clapping in the shadows of the studio theater stopped my answer. From the shadows emerged a tall, pale figure clapping in an exaggerated, slow, but loud manner.

"Very moving," the figure spoke, and then raised his arms leaping fifty feet to the base of the raised stage.

"Evil gets such a bad rap. Evil keeps the world exciting," he hissed and leaped once again into the middle of the stage. The audience gasped and a few screamed and headed for the doors. The rest of the audience stood transfixed by the handsome man with a pale complexion and jet black hair. He sauntered around Oprah waving a bone thin, pale finger at her.

"Shame on you for not inviting an opposing point of view," he said in a hissing voice that exposed long fangs as he circled the talk show host. "I should rip your heart out."

"Stop it. It's me you want," I shouted at him. He stopped and eerily turned eyes the color of blood on me. He was not dressed as the vampires of the horror shows all in black with a cape, but well-dressed in an expensive pair of designer jeans and a tight-fitting tee shirt with a picture of the band Kiss on it.

"Yes, it is you I want," he hissed turning on me.

"No," Dad shouted, moving between the sultry dark being and me.

"No one called you, Dad," the vamp hissed. He grabbed my father by the throat with long fingers capped with extremely long, black nails and threw him into the audience where he landed on several screaming women.

I heard him first. The sound of boards breaking and sheetrock ripping preceded him. I saw him coming from behind the vampire-looking figure. As if he sensed his presence, the vamp turned to face him.

"Pick on me bloodsucker," a transformed Zell said coldly.

Several of Oprah's security personnel arrived trying to remove her from the stage, but she waved them off.

"Help him," she ordered, waving toward Zell. The security turned to face Zell and the vamp and froze. Instead of advancing to help, they slowly, one foot placed vicariously behind another, retreated.

Zell was dressed once again in his light armor, golden hair flowing about his shoulders, a drawn sword in one hand. If I ever had a doubt about goodness and evil, about those of the light and those of the dark, my doubts were now put to rest. Even though Zell's father was evil, Zell was the personification of good. His whole being emanated righteousness while at the opposite end of the spectrum, one could not look at the Dark creature and not shiver from the evil in which he was shrouded. Zell's piercing gaze, now the color of storm clouds, flew briefly to make contact with my blue, frightened ones. From beyond the double studio doors, a rumbling sound echoed. The double doors burst open and a gigantic creature similar to the one in the gym stalked in with a uniformed policeman between his jaws. With a shake of his massive head, the bloodied police officer went flying into the crowd. Panic seized the audience. Screaming, they moved to the perimeters of the room.

The vamp who had turned to watch the arrival of the great beast turned back to Zell. "Let's see how you deal with two of us." He hissed, and Zell drew out his second sword, the metallic sound of it issuing a challenge.

"Do you dare go against the Almighty of Heaven," Zell whispered through clenched teeth.

"Don't be so dramatic Anak. I go against whomever I wish," he laughed.

"It is forbidden!" Zell snarled.

The gigantic wolf creature bound to the stage in three great leaps where it crouched, hovering, and growling at the opposite end from the vampire. Zell moved in an instant positioning himself between the creatures and me. He turned to meet my gaze, and it was as if the world stood still. For that moment, time ceased to exist. Zell was my world and I, his. Lips quivering, I stepped toward him. He bent toward me, gathered me up in one arm, and lifted me off my feet. The tips of our noses touched as we gazed into each other's eyes.

"How very touching," the vamp snapped. "I believe it is love between the beauty and the freak of nature." Zell placed his hand under my chin with the sword still in hand and caressed my face. The creature moved snarling, leaving a trail of bloody saliva as he moved, to meet Zell. The vamp moved in the opposite direction attempting to circle behind us.

Zell reluctantly turned to face the bloodsucker. "From one freak to another, bring it on," Zell spoke so low that only the vamp could hear.

The giant beast leaped at us from the front. Zell moved us, in the twinkling of an eye. The beast landed instead on the vamp causing him to shriek inhumanly. Zell was on him in an instant driving his sword through the back of the beast. The great creature roared snapping, but he could not reach Zell on his back. The monstrous beast still had the vamp pinned to the floor. Zell withdrew his other sword and drove them again and again into the creature. Screaming hideously the creature rolled to its side, and Zell jumped from its back as it did so. The vamp instantly rose stiffly, throwing itself at Zell screeching. The creature raised its head. Oprah grabbed a clipboard from an assistant standing beside her and crashed it down on the creature's great head. I grabbed the hilt of the flaming sword and pulled it from the sheath on Zell's back as he crossed the stage after the vampire. I headed, flaming sword in hand, for the creature. I could hear gasps from the crowd of spectators that huddled against the walls. The creature raised its great head again, and I shoved the flaming sword into one of its great, bloodshot eyeballs. Ghastly shrieks came from the now flaming skull as inch by inch the great creature's body ignited. Withdrawing the flaming sword from the creature, I turned to where Zell and the vamp were locked in a life and death struggle. Once again the vamp's back was to me. Quickly, I crossed the stage and drove the flaming sword into the back of the bloodsucker. The vamp instantly turned on me hissing. Zell grabbed the long, flowing hair of the vamp and pulled its head backward. It screeched and hissed evilly sending strings of bloody saliva projectiles flying from his deadly mouth. Zell used his sword to separate the vamp's head from its body. As Zell held the head by the hair, the rest of the body slumped to the floor. I drove the flaming sword into his chest igniting him. Within seconds, he had burst into flames. Studio personnel rushed to the stage with fire extinguishers.

Oprah held up her hand to stop them, "Let 'em burn," she ordered as she grabbed a microphone from another assistant as she had lost hers in the struggle. Facing the camera with the burning corpses of the vamp and gigantic wolf-like creature in the background she said, "Tomorrow's . . . on tomorrow's show . . . I can't remember who our guest will be tomorrow, but I'm sure it can't top this." With that final word, she thrust the microphone back at the assistant she had taken it from and walked from the stage giving the cut sign to the camera crew.

Dad did not want me to return to New York for the two shows in the morning. I did not agree with him. I had gone this far, and I wasn't about to stop now. The next morning, Zell did not bother to dress in his street clothes. He left the hotel transformed as the Anak. The cab driver recognized us.

"You've got to see this," he said excitedly when Dad and I got in his cab. Zell transformed was much too large to ride in the cab. He hovered about the cab in the air. Instead of heading straight for the television studio, the cabby drove to Times Square. There on almost every billboard was a picture of Zell as the Anak and myself in some form fighting the Dark Ones. There was also brief flashes of a photo of the tender moment we shared on stage. They all read, "Join Annie's Army." As we pulled up outside the studio, crowds wearing "Annie's Army" tee-shirts lined up outside to greet us cheering. Uniformed policemen and members of the S.W.A.T. team were everywhere. Several policemen escorted us into the studio. "We've got your back today, little lady," one of them confided to me. I looked at Zell, and he gave me a warm smile. Every person in the audience had on an Annie's Army tee shirt. I was sure the studio provided them. When Zell, Dad, and I entered the studio, we were given a standing ovation. The host of the show surprised us by showing footage of parents standing in the halls, bathrooms, and classrooms of the local public schools, and of a crowd that had gathered when a lady was injured in an attempted mugging. The crowd had surrounded and held the perpetrator until the police arrived.

"What do you think?" Matt Lauer host of the Today Show asked me.

"I think it's pretty incredible," I answered.

"Had you expected this kind of response to your message on standing up to evil?"

"No, I had hoped for this kind of response but not expected it.

"Will he speak to us?" He asked, looking at Zell, who stood close behind me. I looked to Zell and saw an almost imperceptible shake of the head.

"He rarely speaks to me. I don't think he will." I turned to look at Zell, but I saw his face, appearing stone-like, fixed into a stare, and I knew he would not talk. Just being on television went against everything he had done to remain anonymous, and I knew he made himself vulnerable just for me. "No, he is here to protect me. He won't speak."

We continued to talk about the events of the past few weeks. Several video clips interspersed our conversation: one of the attack at the basketball game, and one was from Oprah's show. But, the one that formed a lump in my throat was the last one that was shown. It was from the attack at the Oprah Show. The clip was when Zell and I had exchanged a brief tender moment before the vampire and the beast had attacked. Even I, in my denial, could see that Zell and I were hopelessly, irrevocably, forever in love. The stark contrast of that tender look as his eyes met mine, and the cold, unseeing eyes he wore just now hit me hard. Though I had experienced that moment, the act of watching our eyes meet, and Zell's gentle caress of my cheek with his sword still clutched in his hand, melted my heart.

"It appears that you two are a couple—a strangely odd couple with him being twice your size, but a couple nonetheless. Can you comment on the relationship that you and this warrior have?"

"We . . . uh . . .we," I began as I searched for words to describe our relationship. "He is my protector and friend, and I am very grateful to him. Though he appears very menacing, at the same time, he is very kind and gentle. I can't imagine my life without him now," I mumbled and blushed as I remembered Zell was here listening to every word.

"What do you hope to get out of this war on evil?" The host asked. I was jolted out of my observations and longings by his comment.

"I don't want to get anything out of it. I just hope people band together, love one another, help their neighbors and friends, and eradicate evil wherever they come across it."

"Where do you go from here?"

I smiled and answered, "I'm going home. I have a basketball tournament to win, a prom to prepare for, and graduation in just a few weeks."

The interview wound to a conclusion minutes later. We received a standing ovation as we left. My restored faith in humanity revived and exhilarated me. We were expected across town at The Early Show within the hour. Several squad cars and a S.W.A.T. team van both led and followed us. The same type of crowd and response met us at The Early Show. I was relieved when it drew to a close and no Dark Ones had shown up. However, from the looks of the hardy spectators in the audience, I had the feeling they were ready for battle and disappointed no monsters made an appearance. We were hurried to a waiting limousine to take us to the airport and home.

❧7.HOMECOMING

WE LANDED AT HARTSVILLE-JACKSON ATLANTA International Airport with our high school band playing and thousands of people wearing Annie's Army tee shirts cheering. I felt like I was the President or a rock star. Every news network and many overseas networks were there sticking microphones in our faces. I wandered over to the crowd and talked to friends and strangers alike. Zell and Dad hovered protectively around me. For the first time in a long time, I felt at home. For the first time since my mother died, I felt at peace. Even though the Dark Ones may kill me tonight, I no longer feared them or death. I knew my mother waited for me. I had not been to school in several days. I wanted to go to school, and a motorcade of police officers escorted me there. It was Friday. All I had to do was stick it out today, and I would have the weekend to recover from the whirlwind of appearances in New York City and Chicago. At Mill Creek High School, students and teachers, also wearing Annie's Army tee shirts, emptied out of the school building and cheered as we climbed out of the patrol cars. Police officers patrolled the halls. Two uniformed officers stood outside the door of the classroom that I was in every class period. They followed me through the halls between classes. I went from being ecstatic to feeling miserable. I didn't need them. Zell had my back.

I still marveled how my life had changed in such a short amount of time. However, it took weeks for my life to return to my new normal. The networks followed me relentlessly hoping to film another attack. Everything was quiet though, and when no attack occurred, they began, one by one, to lose interest and leave town. Life would never return to normal, never return to the way it was before Zell and the Dark Ones arrived, but it did after weeks of cameras, reporters, and police following my every move quiet down some. I should have known we were only in the eye of the storm.

Zell and I spent most weekends at the island fortress to avoid the news media and throngs of people hoping to be there when the next freak show event occurred. Sometimes, my father would accompany us. However, he didn't like the "flight" and opted to stay home most weekends. He trusted Zell completely, and I think he felt I was safer with Zell on the island than in Dacula.

Zell and I arrived at school on Monday after one of those weekends. I remembered as we walked to class that I left my cell phone in Zell's car charging. Zell offered to go back after it, so I sat on a bench under a lofty oak tree watching as he returned to the car. For someone so muscular and large, he had a grace about him that was almost poetic.

If I were a poet, I would write about him. I would write about how his muscles ripple under a loose, flowing shirt that hides his three swords. I would write about how I have run about his feet like an adoring pet just to keep up with the rhythm of his long strides. I would write about how his gorgeous hair floats about his perfect face—hair which would make him the envy of even Hollywood's most glamorous. I would write about his silver eyes, which lock on mine until it seems almost impossible to escape his gaze. I would write about how someone so strong can hold me in the gentlest of embraces. I would write about how his lips feel when pressed gently to mine, and how he has saved my life over and over again. I would write about how it would feel to exist in a world with Zell and without the threat of the Dark Ones.

I was lost in adoring thought as I watched him cross the lawn to the car. In an instant, both our lives changed forever. A white utility van pulled up behind Zell's Lamborghini. Four burly men jumped out of the car. One man pulled something from his pocket and approached Zell from behind as he was leaning in to retrieve my cell phone. Zell went down when the stranger stuck the object to his back. Zell raised his hand to grab on to the Lamborghini's door handle, and another man struck him again. Then a third hit him with an object. Then the fourth. For long seconds it seemed as if Zell was frozen to the handle. Then the men removed the objects and Zell's body went limp. Horrified, it seemed as if I were frozen to the bench. I screamed his name over and over. Finally, I tore myself away and jumped up from the bench running toward him.

Several students were walking to class and stopped to see what was causing all the commotion. Matthew came running to my side. I stopped long enough to tell Matthew what had happened. A look of rage came over his face. As we ran to help him, the four men drug an unconscious Zell to the van. Straining and with great difficulty, they lifted him throwing him inside. Matthew and I ran toward the parking lot, but the van was pulling out as we got there.

"What are we going to do? We have to help him." I yelled frantically out to Matthew.

"Course, we'll help him," Matthew answered, pulling his keys from his pocket. I smiled at Matthew, and we both ran for his truck.

Matthew and I chased the van in his pick-up truck. Neither the van nor Matthew's pick-up truck was made for the chase that ensued. We were far behind, but we managed to keep the van in view in the distance. Every time we gained a little ground, a car would get in our way until we could maneuver around it wasting valuable minutes. The van careened onto the ramp heading for downtown Atlanta.

I felt as though I was going to fall apart. Why Zell? Was it an effort from the Dark Ones to get Zell out of the way in order to get to me? But how would they know his identity? These were human beings that kidnapped him. I had never experienced the Dark Ones using humans to do their dirty work. The one person I could ask if the Dark Ones were ever assisted by humans was traveling quickly away from me in an unknown van.

The white van zipped in and out of traffic making it difficult to keep it in our line of vision. It teetered first one way and then another as the driver spun through traffic. I thought for sure that it was going to flip over when, suddenly, at the last second it pulled on to the West Paces Ferry exit. Trying not to lose the van in traffic, we darted in and out of traffic too making our way toward the exit. I could see it turn east in the distance.

"Matt, take a right at the end of the exit." I was watching the van while Matthew tried to work his way through the thick, tangled Atlanta traffic. Finally, we reached the end of the exit and turned right. The van was nowhere in sight. While we were chasing the van, I had called 911 to report the kidnapping. I dialed the number again to let the police know where our chase had ended. The operator told us to stay put and she would send a police officer to file a report.

Matthew and I drove around looking for the van until a police officer called for us to meet him a few blocks away.

"Do you know of any reason that someone would want to kidnap Mr. Starr," the officer asked in a deep baritone voice.

"Well," I began.

The youngish officer stopped writing and looked at me suspiciously.

"I'm Annie," I explained.

"So?" The officer said rudely as if I were wasting his time.

"As in Annie's Army," I tried lamely to help him make the connection. "He, Zell, is my best friend."

The officer took off his sunglasses and squinted, looking into my face. "Oh, I see," he nodded in affirmation, "and you think someone kidnapped Mr. Starr to get to you?"

"It's a possibility, I know of no other reason why someone would want to harm Zell. He is kind of wealthy though. Maybe, that is the reason. This kidnapping was planned."

"How do you know that?" The officer asked.

"Four men with what must have been Tasers kidnap a six-foot four, very strong young man from a school parking lot. Zell is extremely strong. Even four men could not have kidnapped him unless they rendered him helpless. His kidnappers knew that. They came prepared."

"I see," the officer commented.

"This needs to be handled carefully. If Annie's name gets broadcast all over the news, it could put her life in danger," Matthew pleaded as he pushed his dark hair out of his blue eyes.

After the officer completed his report and left, Matthew and I continued to search the streets for the van. The area was a mix of run down houses and commercial buildings.

"What am I going to do?" I asked looking at Matt.

"We are going to get a map and start searching every parking lot, every backyard and every garage for that van within a ten mile radius of this area," Matthew angrily spouted. "We'll mark each street off as we search them. That van is around here close somewhere. This is not an exit that you get off to get to somewhere else. If you get off at this exit, you have a destination in mind within miles of the exit."

"You're right. Zell is close by. I can feel him," I concurred with Matthew as if in a trance. I wasn't sure what it was, but ever since the blood transfusion, I seemed to have a connection with Zell that was hard to explain—almost other worldly. A few days ago, Dr. Patty talked in biology class about scientists now believing that cells may have memory encoded into them. Perhaps, blood cells do too. Matthew pulled into a convenience store and returned with a city map, a black marker, and a highlighter. He located the exit and outlined a grid with the black marker. We returned to the first street to the right of the exit ramp. Matthew pulled his truck over the curb.

"I'll take the left side of the road and you the right," he nodded in the direction of some buildings that looked to be commercial but exhibited no signs of commerce. "Check around back for the van. If there is a garage, see if you can get in or see in. If it doesn't feel right skip it, we'll come back together to check the building after we finish the street."

I slipped around back of the first building. My heart was beating so loudly that I wasn't sure I would hear Matthew if he called for me. The back of the building contained an abbreviated yard bursting with waist-high weeds. In the very back corner of the property sat a garage of sorts. It looked as though the walls were depending on one another for support. It had been deprived of paint for so many years that its original color was no longer evident. The drive had obviously been overgrown for years as no sign of it was present. I started through the overgrowth carefully.

"I'll probably get a nice case of chiggers," I groaned as I gingerly headed in the direction of the garage. Hopefully, it was too early in the season for chiggers. One pane of glass in the garage was broken out. Wiping away the cobwebs, I peered in the garage. No van. There was only partially decomposed trash littered about. Swiftly, I retraced my steps. I could see the back of the next building, and there was neither garage nor van.

It only took about twenty minutes for Matthew and me to check the buildings and rendezvous back at Matt's truck. We followed the same procedure for hours checking first one street, then another, highlighting them after they were checked.

"Annie, I'm sorry, but I need something to drink. Do you mind if we take a break for a while," Matthew pleaded.

"No, of course not, Matt. You have been great."

Matt and I sat in his truck at a Sonic drinking Cherry Lemonade, resting, and talking.

"What are you going to do if we don't find Zell before it gets dark?" Matthew asked.

"I don't know," I whispered. "I don't know." Matthew sensed that Zell's disappearance made things worse for me, but he didn't know the full extent of the consequences of Zell missing from my life. No one but Dad and I knew Zell was the Annunaki. Perhaps,

Matthew had figured it out. Matt wasn't the sharpest knife in the drawer, so I doubted he knew. I felt if I told him the truth about Zell, it would be a betrayal. Matthew and Zell were friends, but the knowledge that Zell was the Anak may endanger Matthew's life.

"If we don't find Zell today, why don't I get Chris, and we crash at your house tonight. We could get an early start searching in the morning, and if something happens, we'll be there," Matthew offered. I felt relief at the thought of not being alone tonight.

"Matthew, that would be so gr . . ., " I started to say, pausing in mid-sentence.

"Lionel, I must go tell Lionel," I said urgently.

"Who is Lionel?' Matthew asked perplexed.

"He is Zell's assistant," I answered.

"Why does Zell need an assistant?" Matt asked.

"His family owns a cutlery business that has been handed down for generations," I answered. I left out the details that the only 'family' of Zell's still living was a fallen angel father, whom Zell had not seen since he was fourteen when Michael and the Archangels dragged him to hell, or a pit, or somewhere equally horrific.

"Ah, which explains why Zell is somewhat loaded, right?"

"Basically," I answered, shrugging my shoulders ready for this discussion to be over. It felt strange to be discussing Zell's personal life with anyone but him.

Matthew stuck his head out the window and surveyed the clouds forming overhead. "We have two or three hours of daylight left if rain doesn't move in. We better get back to the search." He looked at me and grinned. "We'll find him, Annie."

I flashed a half-hearted grin back at Matthew and leaned my head against the seat closing my eyes. Matthew headed back to where we had abandoned our search and pulled to the side of the road. Carefully, he folded back the map. "We only have half-dozen streets left on the west side of the grid. If we don't find him here, we'll move to the east side." I could tell the neighborhoods were getting more squalid as we made our way further from the interstate. It was a mix of run-down homes, boarded up businesses, and a few sad-looking businesses still open but which looked as though they needed to be boarded up. Matthew opened up his glove compartment and pulled out a magnetic key holder. "Annie, I'm going to put the key to the truck in this magnetic holder and place it just under the tire well on the front driver's side of the truck. Just in case, you get finished searching before me, or . . . if I don't return," Matthew added.

"Don't talk like that Matthew. We're going to find Zell and get out of here," I scolded.

"I just have this feeling things are going to get worse," Matthew murmured, looking out the window at the neighborhood. "Maybe we should hunt together. This place doesn't look too healthy."

"Don't worry about me. If we search together, it will double our search time. Zell may not have that long," I argued.

"Do you think he's been kidnapped for a ransom?" Matthew asked worriedly.

What I couldn't tell Matthew was that even though he didn't know Zell was The Anak, the Dark Ones may. Zell had most likely been kidnapped to get him out of the way so the evil creatures could get to me. That is why time was so urgent.

"I hope so," I murmured. "At least, they will have a motive for keeping him alive if he's being held for ransom."

"See you in a few," Matthew shouted as though I was deaf and slapped the key under the tire well. I sighed, crawled out of the truck, and leaned against it. Matt was right. The atmosphere was different. I surveyed the houses on the side of the street that I was to search. I could tell that at least a half dozen of them did not have a garage or a white van parked in the broken, overgrown lots that surrounded them. Wanting to get the search over, I sprinted for the house on the corner. No garage. The back door and windows were all boarded up. Something had been bothering me for hours. I could feel Zell. I felt as though I was a human GPS. He was close, but not real close. I thought that if I could just search alone that I could find him. Alone was too dangerous, though. Still, the feeling persevered. I looked at the property next door, but I somehow knew he wasn't in there. However, do I take a chance on being this close, and I miss him by going off on some wild goose chase? I must finish looking in this neighborhood first. When Matt and I meet back up, I will tell him what I'm feeling.

I hurdled a low fence that separated this property from the one next door. This property looked as though it had been used in the recent past. There was a fairly new extra-large garage door on the back of the crumbling brick building. I looked around for some way to open it. Seeing nothing, I tried the back door to the building, but it was locked. I noticed what looked to be a basement window peeking out from behind clumps of weeds. I jumped from the back door stoop to investigate the window. I nudged it with the toe of my shoe, and it moved. The window now devoid of paint looked to be about 18 inches long and about a foot high. I thought I should be able to squeeze through. Lying flat on my stomach, I pushed the window which was hinged at the top and stuck my head through to determine how safe it might be to crawl into the basement. From the dim light that filtered through the window, the basement looked harmless enough. Pulling my head from the basement, I swiveled and backed through the window until I was hanging from the window ledge. I knew the floor was only a couple of feet below me, and I took a deep breath and released my grip.

I crouched very still for a few seconds waiting as my eyes adjusted to the darkness in the basement. Things scurried away in the darkness and cobwebs pulled at my hair and clothes. The only light filtered through the window I had just come through. Carefully, I moved to a door that I spied across the room. It groaned and scraped as I shoved it open. The room was basically empty except for a few empty boxes. A staircase stood in the middle of the room. Carefully, I made my way up the creaking stairs. As much as I wanted to find Zell, I hoped the house was empty because I could certainly not sneak up on anyone coming up these stairs. Slowly, I pushed the door at the top of the stairs open and listened. It seemed quiet. Silently, I slipped through the door and into a hallway. Quickly, I moved to a door in the hall and listened again. When I didn't hear anything, I slowly turned the knob. Empty again. I moved silently through the building checking every room. I found the door that led to a big loading dock and the garage, but again, empty. I moved back through the building to where I had seen the back door. I grasped the door knob, but gasped and ducked back behind the wall when I looked out the door.

Down the street where Matthew had left the truck was a creature sniffing around the tires. The sheer size of it made my heart pound so loud that I was afraid the creature would sense my hiding place. The monster evidently picked up my scent and moved slowly head down sniffing toward the first building on the corner that I had checked. For the moment, the creature had his back to me. I would wait. I would wait until the creature got almost to the building on the corner and then I would head for the truck. It would surely follow my scent to this building if I didn't move quickly. I turned the latch on the door as quietly as possible. The door resisted and I moved back to the window to check where the creature was. I was closer to the truck, but the creature was bigger and faster. I needed to get as close to the truck as possible without alerting it. I moved back to the door and pulled again. This time the door grudgingly moved. It made a scraping sound, and I stopped and moved to the window again to check the creature. It was still moving toward the house on the corner with its muzzle close to the ground following my trail. It had not heard the door. Squeezing between the door and the jam, I stepped silently out on the stoop. Watching the monster as I moved, I silently tiptoed down the steps and across the lot. I was shaking so fiercely that I expected the creature to turn and spot me at any moment. However, I kept moving toward the truck. I moved around the back end of the truck and headed to the tire well where Matthew had hidden the key.

I knelt behind the truck and retrieved the key. Peering over the hood of the truck, I looked to where I last saw the creature. It was not there. I dropped behind the truck breathing heavily. Panic seized my chest constricting my breathing. I tried to slow my heaving chest as I peered over the hood of the truck again. It was then that I saw the creature at the basement window sniffing around. Suddenly, the creature stopped and turned its head in my direction. Gasping, I shrunk back behind the trunk.

"I've got to get out of here."

Slowly, the creature took a few steps in the direction of the truck. I pulled the key from the magnetic holder. My hands were shaking so bad the key clattered to asphalt.

"Not again," I whimpered dropping to my knees feeling under the truck where the key had taken a bounce and landed. Closing my hand around the key, I clawed my way up to the door and jammed the key in the lock. Jerking the door open, I grabbed the steering wheel and pulled myself in the truck. The truck started without hesitation. Movement in the rear view mirror caught my attention. The creature was bounding toward the truck. Throwing the truck in gear, I stomped the accelerator leaving the creature behind. Matthew! Where was he? I couldn't leave without him. I blew the horn as I traveled down the street frantically searching for him. Reaching the end of the street, I slammed the truck into reverse backing into a parking lot. I had to go back. I missed Matthew. Pounding on the horn as I went down the street, I searched the buildings for a sign of Matt.

The truck skidded sideways as I slammed on the brakes. There in the middle of the road stood the creature. He lifted his great snout and gave a howl so menacing that I felt the chill begin in my legs and race upward through my body. I began to cry. Not only from the howl, but in the distance, behind the beast, I could see Matthew waving his arms. However, that thing stood between Matthew and me. The creature was so large that it took up most of the road. I would never make it past the monster. If I left, I was sure the creature would follow me and never notice Matthew. He would be safe. I didn't like the thought of leaving Matthew even if it meant saving his life. What if I didn't make it? He may think me a coward or worse—a traitor. There had to be another way.

Squealing tires and burning rubber, I slammed the truck into reverse. As I expected, the giant beast began to chase the truck. I concentrated on driving backwards, and I forgot the monster temporarily as I navigated down the narrow street in reverse. At the end of the road, I stomped the brakes. I shifted into first and took off down a road which intersected with the main road. Turning right onto the highway, I gunned the accelerator for several blocks. My ultimate goal was to work my way back around to where Matthew waited, and hopefully, I would draw the monster away from him.

When I thought I was south of Matthew's position, I made another right turn barely slowing down. Thankfully, there was no oncoming traffic because I was all over the road. One more block and I made another tight right hand turn. I was back on the road where I had last seen Matthew. I slowed down so that I could hunt for him. The creature was nowhere in sight. I saw Matt walking down the middle of the road headed straight for me. Perhaps he had an idea that I led the creature away and would be coming back for him. I sped back up, and he broke into a run when he recognized the truck. I could see the wide grin on his face even from this distance.

Suddenly, his countenance changed, and he bowed his head pumping his arms furiously in a dead run for the vehicle. I glanced to my right through the back window and saw what was responsible for the change in Matt. The monster broke out from between a gap between the buildings and headed for the truck slightly behind and east of the truck. Stomping the gas once again, the creature and I were in a deadly race. I was headed for Matthew. The creature was headed for me. When I passed the gigantic creature, I was close enough to see its red bloodshot eyes. Within seconds, I was at Matt's side. We had only seconds to get Matthew in the truck and get out of here. Matt was on the driver's side of the road, and I threw open the door scooting to the passenger side.

"Let's get out of here!" I screamed

"Done!" Matthew shouted heaving himself in the truck and slamming the truck into gear.

Turning to check on the whereabouts of the creature, I gasped as I saw it leap for the truck just as it lurched forward. The great beast's claws locked on the tailgate for a few seconds, but its great weight ripped the tailgate from the bed of the truck. The enormous monster, tailgate grasped within its great claws, flew backward tumbling, rolling, and landing in a tangled mess with the tailgate. Leaping to its feet, the creature shook its head, lifted its snout to the sky and roared. It was pissed! It took off after us in a dead run.

"It's coming Matt," I yelled over the roar of the engine. Matthew briefly glanced in the rear view mirror, but I could see his concentration was in his turn onto the main road that led to the freeway. I slammed against Matt's shoulder as he swerved onto West Paces Ferry Road. "Sorry," I grunted. Matt lips tried to smile but ended up in a horrid grimace instead. Matt was nearing the entrance ramp for the freeway.

"Do you see it?" He asked venturing a glance in my direction. I turned in the seat and peered out the back window.

"Yeah, it's coming," I answered dully.

"We're almost to the freeway. We can outrun it there," Matt said tersely.

My heart was beating wildly. I could hear it pounding in my ears.

"Hold on," Matt ground out making a screeching, tight right turn onto the entrance ramp sliding sideways. The ramp circled back under the freeway and then entered the freeway once it cleared the overpass. The creature was close. It disappeared as we slid under the overpass. Something rocked the truck slinging me into the dash as we came out from under the overpass. I looked into the bed of the truck and saw the creature trying to right itself. The great beast had leaped from the overpass and landed in the bed of the truck filling it with his enormous size.

"Matt, it's in the truck," I screamed.

Nervously, Matthew watched the creature through the rear view window. "Get my hunting rifle off the rack," Matthew whispered as if the beast might overhear.

I hadn't even noticed that over the back window of Matthew's truck was a double gun rack. In the bottom rack hung Matt's hunting rifle. In the top rack lay Matthew's prized possession, the sword Zell had made for him. Thank God for good ol' Southern boys and their toys. I pulled the rifle from the rack.

"Shoot it," Matthew ordered.

I swung the rifle toward the back of the truck, but the creature was no longer there.

"It's gone," I murmured.

"Gone?" Matthew questioned craning his neck to look briefly into the bed of the truck. We both breathed a sigh of relief. Still grasping the rifle to my chest, I leaned into the back of the seat and closed my eyes.

"For now," I sighed, eyes still closed. "But trouble doesn't leave me alone for long these days."

"Heck, this is the most fun I've ever had in my life," Matthew crowed. "You can hang with me anytime." Despite myself, I had to giggle at Matt's exuberance. My lightened mood disappeared quickly when I heard Matthew let out a screech. Giant claws had him by his left arm attempting to pull him out of the truck. The truck lurched violently from side to side as Matthew attempted to keep control of it. The truck swerved from lane to lane on the interstate. I dropped the rifle on the seat and grabbed the steering wheel attempting to help Matthew.

"No, shoot it!" Matt ground out between clenched teeth. The sleeve of the shirt on his left arm was becoming soaked with blood as Matthew tried to pull his arm from the grasp of the monster. The giant creature jerked in response and Matthew flew from the seat crashing his head against the window sill of the truck. A gash opened up on his forehead and blood trickled down into his eyes while Matthew still maintained his grip on the steering wheel. The truck lurched and the rifle slid into the floor under Matt's feet. "Shoot it," Matthew groaned. "I can't hold on much longer." His gaze went from me to the roof and back again. "Shoot it."

I slid from the seat and reached under Matt's knees to retrieve the rifle, but it was wedged underneath the accelerator. "I can't get it out Matt," I cried. Just as the words left my mouth, I saw the gleaming sword still cradled in the rack. Half leaping back into the seat, I jerked the sword from the rack and slid it from its lovely sheath. I plunged it deep into the lower arm of the creature. A mammoth shriek rocked the truck as the creature released Matthew and attempted to pull his arm from the sword. I held the sword tight as Matt gained control of the crazily swaying truck. With a great tearing sound, the creature pulled back his arm and unskishkabobed himself from the sword. An otherworldly shriek joined the sounds of interstate traffic as the monster bellowed his unhappiness with the turn of events. I could see motorists and their gaping stares in my peripheral vision. Some started blasting away on their horns. I imagined they were trying to be helpful and scare the creature away. I knew it wasn't going anywhere. This was a fight to the death. I just hoped it wouldn't be ours. Matthew managed to kick the rifle free from underneath the accelerator with the toe of his left shoe.

Once again I dropped into the floor, this time successfully retrieving the rifle. Cocking the barrel, I jammed the nozzle of the gun against the ceiling of the truck, turned my head, closed my eyes, and pulled the resisting trigger. The deafening noise of the firing rifle exploded inside the truck. The shriek that followed made the previous one seem like a whimper. The huge beast landed with a bone-crunching thud on its back in the bed of the truck. It lay there breathing heavily with a gapping, torn hole in its chest. Slowly, the creature's breathing slowed and finally stopped. Matthew and I were both covered in blood splatters and bits of leathery flesh from the monster.

"Whew," Matt sighed. "That was awesome!"

I smacked Matt's good arm and said, "You're insane." Matt turned and flashed me a goofy grin. I sat the rest of the way to Dacula on my knees with the rifle aimed at the creature out the back window of the truck. I watched the innate body of the monster.

"Do you think it's dead?" I asked Matthew.

Matthew half turned in his seat and peered through the back window.

"Looks like it to me."

"We have to go tell Lionel that Zell is missing," I stated as I gave Matthew directions to Zell's home on Lake Lanier. Forty minutes later, I stood at Zell's door ringing the bell. Matthew was at the bed of the truck poking the creature with the barrel of the rifle like a child who pokes a stick at a burning ember of a fire.

Lionel opened the massive door and greeted me. "Good evening, Miss Annie." He nodded and gave a slight bow at the waist.

"May I come in Lionel? I need desperately to talk to you."

"Of course, Miss Annie. Will your friend join us?" He asked nodding in Matthew's direction.

"I don't know. He's guarding the body of a Dark One. We're not sure it's dead."

"I see," Lionel answered evenly slightly raising his right eyebrow. "Let's make sure that it is." Lionel flipped a switch by the front door and the fire pit to the side of the house that overlooked the lake lit up. He grabbed a silver pistol in an ornate holster that lay inside the drawer of a beautiful mahogany table beside the door and wrapped it around his waist buckling it. He lifted a sword tucked into an ornate sheath from the wall and headed for the truck.

At the bed of the truck, he peered over the side at the dark creature. "Hmm, quite the creature you have bagged there, Miss Annie." He took the gun from its holster and poked the creature. No movement. He looked at Matthew and then at me.

"I'm sorry Lionel. This is Matthew. He is a friend of mine and Zell's. Zell has been taken. We were looking for him when this creature attacked."

"I see," Lionel stated calmly grabbing the creature by its bloody, hairy shoulder and dragging it from the bed of the truck. "Master Matthew, would you be as good as to assist me? I want to drag this creature to the fire pit and toss him in."

"Cool, bring on the marshmallows and weenies," Matthew crowed enthusiastically grabbing the creature by the other shoulder. Together Lionel and Matthew drug the Dark One to the side of the huge fire pit and rolled him in. His scruffy hair immediately blazed up. Within minutes the entire body of the Dark One was ablaze.

"We'll watch and wait, "Lionel began when a horrific howl came from the ball of fire that was attempting to climb out of the pit. Lionel and Matthew both took aim and emptied their guns into the fireball that was the Dark One. The immense creature staggered backwards into the pit once again. Lionel drew the sword from the sheath and with one blow separated the creature's smoking head from his body. This time the Dark One succumbed to his fiery demise.

"Wow, Annie! I love hanging with you. There is never a dull moment." Matthew said proudly as if it was an honor instead of a death wish to be my friend.

"Quickly, follow me into the house," Lionel insisted. We followed Lionel up the path to the house. Just inside the door, Lionel pulled on a picture frame. It swung open like a well-oiled safe revealing a series of switches and buttons. Lionel flipped the first switch, and I heard something heavy slam into place outside the door. Switches two, three, and four hurled steel plates in front of the windows in the great room from the outside.

"Miss Annie and Master Matthew would you assist with the other two windows?" Lionel walked to the closest window, pulling down a metal panel that adorned the top of the windows. I had thought them to be decorative as they were carved in the same ancient writing as Zell's swords and the massive front door. The steel panel slid easily over the inside of the window and locked into place. Lionel pulled a steel bar from behind the sophisticated draperies swinging it across the steel panel securing it in place with a steel pin also hidden behind the opposing drapery. He nodded to Matt and me, and we both followed his example locking in steel plates over the remaining windows in the great room while Lionel moved to the fireplace and built a roaring fire. He rose from the hearth of the massive fireplace and dusted off his hands. "There, no Dark Creature will dare challenge that fire."

"Follow me," Lionel ordered. We followed him to the dining room and kitchen and repeated the same procedure there for the few windows in those rooms. Lionel threw switches which slammed steel plates over the windows from the outside, and then we three slid steel plates over the inside of the windows. I was beginning to feel safer by the minute. "Now, we need to go into the Master's bedroom. Master Matthew bring your rifle."

Matthew retrieved his rifle off the great mahogany table just inside the door and followed Lionel disappearing into Zell's bedroom behind him. Not wanting to be alone in the great room, I trotted after them. Lionel crossed the room to a massive entertainment center which housed an expansive flat screen television, a multitude of books, and some ancient looking artifacts. Lionel pulled out a book on the end and slid his hand in the empty pocket that the book had previously occupied. There was a snap and the entertainment center began to move from the wall. Behind the entertainment center was a metal door hidden in the wall. Lionel pulled a key from his pocket and unlocked the door. Matthew and I followed Lionel through the door into a steel plated room that was furnished immaculately with a day bed at one end piled with decorative pillows. On either side of the day bed were two overstuffed leather chairs with matching ottomans. A refrigerator, sink, microwave, and another door through which I could see a full bath was situated at the other end of the room making the room entirely self-sufficient. The left wall was floor to ceiling cabinets filled with plastic dishes, cutlery, cans and boxes of vegetables, canned meats, and fruits. The opposite wall was lined with gun and weaponry cabinets. There were a variety of pistols, rifles, shotguns, swords, and knives displayed in multiple cabinets.

"Spectacular," Matt breathed heavily. Lionel pulled open a drawer in one of the gun cabinets and pulled out a box of shells.

"These should work in your rifle," Lionel said, handing the box of bullets to Matthew. Matthew reloaded his gun and tried to give Lionel back the rest of the box. Lionel refused shaking his head.

"Keep the box. You may need them." Lionel chose an automatic pistol and pulled a box of clips out of the drawer and shoved them into my arms. "Load this one for yourself."

I hesitated, but hadn't I just shot a creature perched atop Matthew's truck? I knew I would use it to save Zell, Matthew, or myself if it came to that. Lionel picked out an Uzi and double-barreled shotgun for himself and headed for the door.

"Follow me," Lionel ordered and left the room. He headed for the great room again and laid his gun and box of bullets on the mahogany table next to the door. He flipped up a large wooden rectangle hidden in the polished mahogany wood floor. Moving back to the switch box hidden behind the picture, he flipped a switch from the box behind the picture. A steel plate slowly dropped down from the ceiling and locked in place sealing off the door. Lionel turned to us.

"Have a seat beside the fire, and I'll have Cook fix us something to eat. I'll also tend to Master Matthew's wounds. Those Dark Ones can be nasty creatures," he coolly said and walked across the room like a man with a purpose and a mission disappearing into the hallway that led to the kitchen. Matthew and I looked at each other in wide-eyed wonder.

"This place is a fortress," Matthew said in wonder as he moved around the room lovingly caressing the metal plates that secured the windows and doors.

"I think Zell may have had an idea this day would come," I said, sinking into the couch with a sigh. I was exhausted. Matt and I had searched for Zell since early this morning, and then there was the fight with the Dark Creature in the truck. I leaned my head back into the plush couch and closed my eyes. I must have fallen asleep for a few moments. The next thing I knew when I opened my eyes again, Lionel was finishing up bandaging Matthew's wounds. An elderly lady was just sitting down two trays on the massive coffee table. Two small, delicate looking steaks sat alongside tender stalks of asparagus, a steaming bowl of soup, plump rolls, a mug of coffee, and a glass of iced tea adorned each tray. Lionel slid one tray on the coffee table in front of me and the other in front of Matthew.

"Please eat while I speak with you," Lionel generously offered. He waited until Matthew and I began eating before he began. "Master Starr built this home knowing full well a day similar to this may come. He is quite wealthy you know, and there are those who would do him harm," Lionel glanced briefly at me letting me know this story was for Matthew. Both sides and the back of this structure are built into the rock wall of the bluff. The only point to be defended is the front of the home. All windows and doors, even the garage doors, can be covered inside and out with steel plates. The frame of the house is all steel. Floors, ceilings, and sides of this home are virtually impenetrable. Inside Master

Starr's bedroom suite is a safe room, the room we just retrieved our weapons from. If for some reason the Dark Ones should gain entry to the house, you two will go to the safe room. Under the day bed is a tunnel. The switch to move the bed and open the hatch to the tunnel is on the left inside the door of the gun cabinet. You will come to the end of the tunnel in the boathouse on the lake. Next to the switch in the gun cabinet is a set of keys. One of the keys is to a boat. Inside the boathouse, there is a boat that the key fits. Take the boat; keep it to the right of the lake. In about a mile you will see a dock with a flag of two crossed swords. Pull into that boathouse. There is a Hummer parked in there which you may use to escape. The key to the Hummer is on the key chain with the boat key. Inside the glove box, there are instructions on where to find several safe houses throughout the world. There are alternate identifications, cash, and credit cards in the glove box for you to use. Mr. Starr has given much thought into where you should go if something happens to him. Follow the directions in the glove box. Do not go home under any circumstances. Make your way to a safe house. The keys to all of them are on the keychain. There is also an extra set in the glove box. There are sufficient funds to get you anything you need. Do not make the mistake of returning to your homes. The Dark Ones will go there to find you. If it is possible for Mr. Starr to follow you, he will find you at whichever one you choose to go. Do you have any questions?"

Somewhere during this discourse I had ceased to eat and sat there with my mouth open in some state of shock. I looked over at Matthew. He, too, sat there fork dangling in midair, mouth open. The usually verbal Matthew was speechless. We both were jolted back into the present by a loud banging on the outside metal plate on the door. Lionel casually walked to the coffee table and picked up remote to the television. He turned it on and there on the television was Kate and Christopher banging at the metal plate yelling.

"Annie, Matt, are you two in there?" Kate turned and screamed as she stared into the darkness. There, just beyond her I could see two familiar red and yellow eyes glowing in the darkness. Immediately I jumped up and ran for the door.

"We got to help them. We've got to let them in."

"No," Lionel shouted.

"Yes," I yelled back. I didn't sign up for this to watch my friends die. I haven't been talking for weeks about standing up to evil wherever it finds me to let them die on the other side of this door."

"Annie go to the safe room and lock yourself inside, and I will let them come in," Lionel said in desperation. "If we don't come for you in five minutes, leave. Go through the tunnel to the boathouse. Promise me, and I will let them in. Perhaps, you should go too, Master Matthew."

"No way. Those are my friends out there. I'm staying."

I looked at the screen again. Kate was screaming and pounding on the door. I could tell the red and yellow eyes were getting closer.

"Go Annie," Matthew urged.

"They are my friends too," I half sobbed.

"I know," Matthew spoke gently, "but Lionel won't let them in if you stay."

"I'll go. Save them." I half sobbed and ran for Zell's room. I didn't want to go, but Kate and Christopher didn't have time for me to test Lionel's resolve to leave the door unopened. I ran through the still open door to the safe room, hit the switch on the inside which closed the door and moved the bookcase back to its original position. I stood staring at the door, breathing heavily, for what seemed to be an eternity. How long had it been? I hadn't looked for the time when I entered the room. I crossed the room to where the television remote was lying and pushed the button to check the time. Instead of a guide, movie, or program coming on, a picture of the outside of the house popped onto the screen. It stayed there for a few seconds. Then a picture of the kitchen area popped up, followed by pictures of the great room, another view of the outside, the boathouse, the dock, and other rooms in the house. I could see Lionel, Matthew, and Christopher were battling a creature in the great room. Furniture was overturned, pictures were off the wall and smashed, and draperies were shredded into pieces. All the other rooms were empty. I wondered where Kate was. Fingers of panic grabbed and squeezed until my chest hurt. Another view of the outside of the house came on the screen, and there by the front door a shadowy figure stood. The camera switched to the fight in the great room, then the kitchen. I picked up the remote pushing buttons. I wanted the screen to go back to the great room. I pushed a button, and the camera went back to the front door, and I jumped back. Standing there staring at the camera with a creepy smile was a man, a sinister-looking man. There was something familiar about him. As if in a trance, I moved closer to the screen.

"Let me in, Annie," the figure pleaded. "It's no use, you know. We'll get to you sooner or later. Save your friends. Come, let me in." It was as if I was paralyzed. I knew him. I knew his voice. I had known a face similar to this one. It was Jon. Jon was peering into the camera with a sinister look on his face. His pointed teeth shone in the light of the porch. His blue eyes were now a dark mass. A shiver went down my spine. "Annieeeee," Jon cooed. "Annie, all I want to do is turn you to the Dark Side.

They'll stop hunting you if that happens. *They* don't want Kate, Chris, and Matt, but if they get in your friends will be collateral damage. We do want him though. We want to cut off his head. He won't look so hot in pieces, will he? Is he in there with you?"

Just then the door to the safe room swung open. I inhaled deeply and was crushed by two arms going around my neck. It was Kate.

"Shut the door, quickly," sobbed Kate, "one of those things got into the house before Lionel could get the door shut. He told me where you were. He said to get in here and tell you to head for the boathouse."

"No, I can't leave Matthew, Lionel, and Christopher."

"You have to Annie. Otherwise, their sacrifice is in vain," Kate whispered holding me close. She looked around the room. I imagined she looked for the way to the boathouse.

"What do you mean sacrifice? Are they. . .?"

I looked back as the monitor switched back to the outside. Jon was leaning against a porch post surveying long, deadly looking fingernails. Behind him was darkness. A storm must be brewing outside because a sudden lightning strike near the lake showed darkened figures everywhere.

"No, at least not when I left the room. Annie, you have no choice. You must survive. Lionel said that if you come in there that *thing* will come for you immediately, and he doesn't know if they can stop it. They are filling it full of lead. Hopefully, it will work," Kate replied almost yelling.

"Why must I survive? At the expense of my friends, I don't think so." I answered stubbornly.

"Annie, you must live. You must find Zell. Only you can find him."

"Zell?" At the mention of Zell, I felt my legs go weak. I don't know how she knew, but I was sure she was correct. All day while we were searching, I was drawn in a different direction. Matthew wanted to finish searching the west side of Paces Ferry Road before we moved to the east side, but I felt as though I was being drawn east. The feeling had become stronger throughout the day. We were almost finished searching the west side, so I waited. Then, we were chased by the dark creature, and we gave up the search early.

"Annie, we need to go," Kate said, bringing me back to reality. I shook my head to clear the fog that seemed to pervade it. I took two great strides and pummeled the switch to the hidden passage with my fist. I suddenly wanted to live to find Zell. I was probably the only person alive that was capable of finding him. The bed slowly tilted on its side until it lay flat against the back wall. I grabbed the keys that Lionel had described, and Kate and I moved from the side of the bed to the steps that descended underground. Lights covered in steel rails lit the way. Kate stepped on the first step and reached back to take my hand. Together, we hurried down the steps. We went down about thirty steps when they ended into a stone foyer.

Lionel warned me to look for the switch which would put the bed back in place, and I quickly found it. The bed gave a humming sound as it returned to its original position. A muffled thud assured me that the bed was locked back into position. It seemed eerie standing in this stone foyer when my friends were above us battling for their lives. I turned to face a small metal door that obviously led to the tunnel Lionel spoke of. Taking a deep breath, I moved the steel bar from in front of the door and swung the door open. Lights began to come on lighting the tunnel. Kate stepped through the door into the tunnel and pulled me after her. She turned and shut the door sliding a steel bar in place to shut off the door to anyone who may follow us. I was torn by her actions. What if Lionel tried to follow or Matthew and Christopher? Again, what if a Dark One found his way into the Safe Room and tried to follow us?

We followed the tunnel in eerie silence. "Kate, why did you and Chris come out to Zell's lake house?" I asked suddenly curious.

Kate shrugged her shoulders. "Chris and I were hanging out. We were working on some Calculus problems when Chris received a text from Matthew that you two may need some help finding Zell. Chris and I never knew he was lost. He said you two were here. Let me see, work on Calculus or go see what adventure Matt and Annie has going on. Duh, no brainer, of course we slammed the book shut and headed out here. We had no idea there would be such an interesting welcoming party. But hey, I should've known. You have been having way too much fun lately."

I gave a half-hearted laugh, but my voice echoed creepily back to me. Moss grew on the stones in this part of the tunnel muffling the sounds, and there was the sound of dripping water. This setting was straight out of a horror movie. I figured we must be getting close to the lake. The tunnel ended in a pool of water.

"You've got to be kidding me. Really?" I groaned. Lionel forgot to mention we had to swim for our lives.

"I guess that's one way to hide an entrance to a secret passage—submerge it. I bet those hairy things and vamps don't do water," Kate laughed plopping down and pulling off her tennis shoes.

"You're going in there?" I asked Kate dubiously.

"Why not? I know what's in the direction we just came." Kate giggled.

"Good grief," I moaned, pulling off my sandals and stuffing them down my shirt. "These shoes cost me a hundred dollars. I may live through this night, but I'm not sure about my shoes. Lead the way," I told Kate. She turned and gave me a curt smile, then dove into the water. I dove in after her. We swam only about eighty feet when I saw a light above the water, Kate headed for the light, and I was right behind her. When my head broke the water, I saw we were inside of a building. Turning, I spied a boat about ten feet away in one direction and a ladder in the other direction. I swam for the ladder and pulled myself out of the water. Kate did likewise. We were sitting on a wooden walk catching our breath when Kate poked me in the ribs.

"Take a load of that," she said, pointing at the boat. There in beautiful letters was the name Annie written on the side of the boat. I felt a lump catch in my throat and tears spring to my eyes. I was the only thing Zell ever had on his mind. It must have been that way for hundreds, maybe thousands of years. Somehow, I was beginning to believe his incredible story. How could he have possibly felt? Zell had no family. How was he able to keep going on through his extended life waiting for the one that he was destined to be with and protect?

I was roused from my thoughts by Kate tugging on my hand.

"Come on." What did Lionel say you should do once you get to the boathouse?"

"Ummm, he said to take the boat and keep right until I see a flag with crossed swords. There will be another boathouse with a Hummer inside. I am to take the Hummer and go to a Safe House Zell has prepared."

"Let's go." Kate said.

I pulled my sandals from my wet shirt and slipped them on. Pulling the boat key from my jeans pocket, I stood up and followed the wooden walk to the side of the boat my shoes squishing all the way. Kate and I climbed in pulling the rope off its mooring. I pushed the throttle forward, and we slowly left the boathouse. I looked back toward the house, but everything was dark except for a small fire that must have been the remains of the Dark One burning in the fire pit. The house looked so far away. Did my friends still live? Shivering, I accelerated and turned the boat to the right. I hung to the right shoreline, and within ten minutes, I saw the crossed swords flag flapping in the night wind. Turning the motor off, I sat in the boat and listened. Chilled, I felt as though I was being watched.

"Come on," Kate urged. "This place feels creepy."

"My whole world has turned into a Creep Fest," I groaned. We jumped out on the dock and tied the boat to a wooden pillar. Cautiously, we approached a small garage that had a garage opening to dry dock a boat and another garage door on the opposite end. There was a single light over a walk-through door on the side of the building from which light spilled over onto the dock. Kate approached the door and tried the handle. It opened easily. Silently, she slipped through the opening closing the door behind her.

"Kate," I whispered when she didn't return. "Kate?" I turned the knob on the door, and it swung open. Bright lights hurt my eyes as they popped on.

"Hard to find the switch in the dark," Kate laughed.

"You scared me silly."

"Nah, you were already silly," Kate laughed. "Lookee here," she whistled. My eyes slowly focused on what appeared to be a Hummer on steroids. It was jacked up with shiny, heavy-duty grills on the front and the back. Multiple layers of thick armor plating were riveted on virtually every surface. There was a small turret on top with openings that looked like it might have been made for guns.

Kate pulled on the door of the Hummer. "It's locked," she groaned hitting the side of the car in frustration.

"I have the key," I held the ring with the boat and Hummer key up for her.

"Excellent," she laughed.

We slid into the Hummer and started the engine. I hit the remote on the visor, and the garage door slowly opened. I pulled out of the boat house and stopped for a moment to hit the remote again to close the door. Suddenly, the door flew open, and I was pulled from the vehicle. Standing above me stood a tall creature with great pointed ears cropped and swept upward. Their directions were mirrored by the upsweep of two thin knobby curling horns that protruded from the top of the creature's head. Sharp, pointed teeth with uneven lengths threatened as the creature hovered above me hissing. I lay on the ground at the beast's feet shaking from terror. A huge, prodigiously pointed tongue hung from between the monster's jagged teeth. An enormous nose spread across the creature's face much like that of a great ape. Massive brows protruded and outlined small, beady red and yellow eyes which watched me. Kate was out of the Hummer and around the vehicle in seconds. She held a crossbow in her hand and threatened the monster.

"Leave it to Zell to fully equip a vehicle," she laughed at me, and then turned back to the Dark One. "Hey, you big, ugly, sweaty excuse for a monster," Kate yelled while shaking her weapon at the great beast.

"Kate, don't . . . run," I yelled back. The monster's gaze who had turned on Kate returned to me. His great mouth opened and a threatening growl emanated from him. I searched for the gun Lionel gave me. I either left it in the safe room or lost it in the water.

"Oh, no you don't," Kate yelled again running toward the creature shooting the creature in the side. She quickly reloaded again and landed another arrow within centimeters of the first. "Get in the car Annie and go."

The creature roared and turned to face Kate. "Never, Kate." Even as I yelled an answer to Kate, she began to change before my eyes. Her clothes strained against an ever increasing body. Material ripped and stretched until only shreds of it covered her. My dear friend, Kate, metamorphosed before my eyes. Not only did she greatly increase in stature, but her face took on an ethereal, marble look. Her long golden hair blew gently around her body. Her eyes flashed and shone like two beacons. This creature was not my friend Kate. She was absolutely frightening. I was mesmerized. She looked like the female counterpart for Zell in his Anak transformation. Kate, this Kate, was stunningly celestial. She must have stood nine feet tall. Her skin glowed like there were lights in the dermis layer underneath the epidermis layer of skin. She held a crossbow in her hands and a sword through the loop of the remains of her jeans compliments of Zell's arsenal in the vehicle. I was in the process of getting up as she drew the creature's attention away from me and to herself. The shock of seeing my childhood friend transform into this fearsome angel made my knees shake and weaken. I slumped back to the ground. The monster roared again and charged Kate. Great white and golden wings sprang from Kate's back and with one great swish she flew high out of the creature's grasp. In a sort of demonic imitation, the creature's gnarled back produced a hideous pair of knobby, blackened wings. With a swish of those grotesque wings, the creature leapt from the ground and met Kate in the air. With a bone-crunching thud, they met in midair where lightning sparked from their collision. Kate drew her sword and thrust it into the belly of the creature. The creature roared and slashed Kate with razor-sharp claws. Blood flowed and ran down Kate's cheek and arm, but as I watched the gaping wounds closed and healed themselves. The creature turned and lunged for me, but Kate threw herself on its back. She grabbed the creature by a knobby horn and pulled its grotesque head back and sunk a dagger in its chest. The creature gargled a scream and attempted to free itself from Kate's grasp. Kate held on and rode the convulsing creature like a bronco.

I could not believe my eyes. I sat back on my haunches transfixed by the scene before me. My best friend was a warrior angel, and I had never known— never even guessed. Why was Kate revealing herself now? Kate pulled the jewel-encrusted dagger from the creature's body and drove it deep into the creature's neck. The creature screeched and rolled trying to dislodge Kate from his back. Kate and the monster melted together, becoming a bloody blur contorting, falling, fighting, slashing, and rolling over and over on the ground. I opened my eyes and spied her sword lying only a few feet from her. Looking back to Kate, I saw the creature turn and sink its long teeth into Kate's shoulder and neck. I crawled on my knees toward the sword, grasped the hilt in both hands and tried to stand.

"This sword must weigh fifty pounds," I groaned. I drug it and moved in the vicinity of the deadly struggle between Kate and the creature. It was difficult to tell where my friend Kate ended and the monster began. Blood flowed freely blurring the distinctions between friend and foe. The great beast shook his head causing Kate to groan and toss about still impaled on his great teeth.

"Finish him," whispered Kate opening her eyes and allowing me to tell where her face was in the sea of red. I almost fainted. I could tell now that half of my friend from shoulder to chin was within the mouth of the great beast. The Dark One had forgotten me in its deadly struggle with Kate. Anger rose up in me. This evil creature was harming my lifelong friend, Kate. If I didn't do something, she, warrior angel or not, was about to die. The beast had rolled on top of Kate presenting its backside to me and was shaking Kate in a deadly grip. I raised the sword as high as I could manage and thrust the sword through the back of the creature's neck. The Dark One and Kate both screamed. The creature released Kate, but she still clung to him even as he thrashed about.

"Annie, pull me off of him," Kate cried out. I looked and could tell the sword had gone clean through the great beast's neck coming out the front side and into Kate's shoulder pinning her to the beast. Slipping my arms around Kate, I gently pulled her off the sword and the creature. "Awwga," Kate groaned. I sank to my knees and put Kate's head in my lap. I pulled off my shirt and wiped blood from her face.

"I'm sorry, Kate," I sobbed.

"For what?" Kate whispered.

"For getting you into this," I sobbed louder burying my face against the bloody face of my friend.

"Hey, what are friends for," Kate tried to laugh, but only succeeded in spitting up blood. "Finish him off," Kate choked as projectiles of blood shot out of her mouth.

"What?" I asked.

"Finish him off. You must cut off his head and burn him—quickly. He's an eternal. It is the only way to finish him. He'll heal and wake up soon if you don't," Kate urged. I looked from Kate to the Dark One and back to my friend. "Do it," Kate ordered. I wadded my bloody shirt into a pillow and gently laid Kate's head upon it. I rose to my feet and moved to the side of the beast which was still moving. I grabbed the hilt of the sword with both hands and pulled. The sword resisted at first. Putting a sandaled foot on the creature's head, I pulled with all my might.

"I'm definitely going to trade these sandals in for combat boots," I huffed. The sword moved a few inches, then stopped. Determined, I continued to pull. It moved a few inches a second time, and then gave way all at once. It slid swiftly from the body of the Dark One sending me sprawling on my back. I jumped up quickly, fearing the creature would be upon me at any second.

Breathing heavily, I was moving only on adrenaline which had been running high all day, Exhaustion consumed me. I searched and searched for Zell, ran from the Dark Ones, swam through a cold lake, and my strength was about gone. Staggering, I drug the heavy sword behind me and placed it against the Dark One's neck.

"Please help me," I prayed silently, closed my eyes, and lifted the sword. I brought it down against the creature's neck rapidly with the assistance of gravity. The Dark One hissed at me sending streams of bloodied saliva in my direction as its grotesque head separated from its body. I threw the sword from me and headed for the Hummer. I pushed in the lighter on the dash and searched for something to burn while it heated. Cramming my hand down in my jeans pocket, I felt a piece of paper. Pulling it out, I realized it was my Calculus homework from this morning. If I burned it, I would have to do the assignment over as I never made it to class today. This morning seemed decades ago.

"Such a high price to pay," I sighed, lighting the homework and tossing it on the carcass of the creature. I gathered dry leaves, pine needles and small sticks to fuel the flames and soon had a small bonfire. The smell was horrific. It smelled of sulfur and rotten eggs. These Dark Ones smelled as horrid as they looked. When I was satisfied that the beast was toast, I searched for Kate. She was gone.

"Kate," I screamed into the night. I ran around to the opposite side of the Hummer looking for her. "Kate," I screamed again, sobbing now. A pair of headlights appeared from a bend in the road. As I watched, a vehicle roared to a stop before me. I reached for the sword I had thrown down. I swung it before me threatening the vehicle that had come to rest in front of me. Doors on both sides of the vehicle opened. I sunk to my knees with relief when Matthew, Lionel, and Christopher emerged from the vehicle.

"Thank you God," I struggled to my feet and screamed as I ran for my friends jumped into their arms and returned their hugs." I can't find Kate," I sobbed. "She fought the creature," I gestured toward the burning mass, "and then, she disappeared."

"Are you hurt, Miss Annie?" Lionel asked, rushing to my side.

"I don't think so," I answered still sobbing. "But, Kate . . ."

"There she is," Matthew yelled. I turned to look in the direction Matthew was pointing, and I saw Kate emerge from the water. At first, only the top of her head peeked through the dark, churning water. Slowly, she rose. She was washed clean of the blood, but her clothes were still in shreds. I jumped up, ran to her, and threw my arms around her wet body. It was Kate, not the pumped up angel version, but Kate, my best friend.

"Annie, what just happened, it's our secret," Kate whispered in my ear.

I knew what she meant and smiled through my tears in response. "I was so afraid when you disappeared that I had lost my dearest friend in the world."

"I needed a minute," she whispered giving me a cock-eyed grin. "I had a little cleaning up and healing to do before anyone saw me." It was then I noticed that though her clothes were still in shreds, she had no bite marks or wounds. However, there were many ugly, reddish marks like skin just healed. She was healed from the wounds the beast had inflicted. I stared at her in bewilderment.

"How?" I asked.

Kate glanced over to where Lionel, Matthew and Christopher were watching the Dark One burn. "Have you never heard of guardian angels?" Kate asked. "I was handpicked by the Ancient One and sent to you years ago by the archangels Michael and Gabriel." Kate still whispered low enough that the guys standing around the burning creature could not hear.

"If you are an angel, why did you leave me in the school parking lot that night?"

"I thought it was time you and Zell met." Kate grinned mischievously. "I am forbidden to interfere as long as Zell is around. There has been a pact between the Dark Ones and the Angels from eons ago that only one Dark Angel can be sent to do its evil. You know of the world wars and the atrocities that have happened in the past. They were all created by hordes of the Dark Ones and Angels fighting each other. Wars are simply a by-product of heavenly and hellish clashes. Clashes so violent that they spill over on mankind creating conflicts and all sorts of evil until it was forbidden by the Almighty. Now only one Dark One is allowed to hunt a human and only one angel is allowed to protect that human at a time. I thought it was time you were introduced to Zell, who has been secretly protecting you all your life. I knew he was there that night just as I could feel the Dark One's presence when we left the gym."

"But Zell is an Anak not an angel," I argued.

"Zell is more angelic than he knows," Kate smiled. "He was conceived of a great evil thrust upon humans by the Dark Angels, but Zell never succumbed to the Dark Side. He has always, for thousands of years, fought on the side of the light through his own sheer will. The Ancient One smiles upon him."

I fought back tears at the thought of Zell. I knew he didn't believe that. He thought himself cursed by his paternity. Where was he? Is he alive? My thoughts were interrupted by Matt and Chris.

"Oh baby," Christopher cooed teasingly at Kate's wardrobe disarray, "You must have given that mutt a heck of a fight."

"Oh, she did. She was fabulous!" I gushed appreciatively.

Chris gave me a strange look and only then did I realize I was standing there in my sports bra having taken off my shirt to soak up the blood from Kate's body. Kate held up my soaking wet shirt.

"Thanks. I used it to wash up," she grinned in a sly, apologetic smile. I wrung the shirt out the best I could and slipped it back on.

"We need to get back to the house," Lionel urged. "We are very vulnerable out in the open. Get into our vehicle, and I'll return the Hummer to the boathouse." Within minutes, Lionel was back in the vehicle, and we headed back for the house. When we arrived at the main road, we made a right turn. The drive to Zell's house was only a half a mile down the road, and we were quickly there. The driveway turned right into a forest of trees. Then, the drive opened up to nine acres of cleared and immaculately landscaped lawn with the house sitting next to the lake and a rock bluff at the back of the property. As the vehicle left the trees, the sight before us chilled my blood. Kate gasped. I heard Matt and Chris swearing under their breath, and I could almost hear Lionel grinding his teeth together.

There were Dark Ones everywhere. Most were in a dark angelic form. Winged creatures, Dark Angels, forbidding, dark silhouettes stood every few feet, leaving only the driveway clear. There must have been hundreds of them. Some were in the form of beasts growling low, deep, throaty growls, but most were enormous, dark, winged angels that turned to watch us as we slowly drove past. It was beyond terrifying.

"Why don't they attack?" Matthew whispered.

"From what I have been told only one Dark One is allowed to attack at a time. Many hundreds of years ago, they attacked in unison, but the turmoil flowed over into humanity. God, Himself, has forbidden the Dark Ones to attack humans or angels except for a one on one basis. That is what holds them. That being said, which one will attack now?" Lionel groaned as he finished relating the same story that Kate had just revealed to me.

Even as he finished, a great, winged creature rose from the roof of the house and flew straight for us. Lionel stomped the gas and a malevolent roar went up from the ungodly host that surrounded us. Lionel hit the garage door opener just as the creature hit the windshield causing tiny cracks to stream in every possible direction from the impact point. I could see the winged creature vividly. It had the form of an angel, but it had the face of a demon. It was a deep burgundy color and had a tail with a trident shaped point at the end. The pupils of its eyes were yellow, but the sclera, what would have been the white part of the human eye, was a deep, blood red. The creature clawed at the window trying to break its way through. Matthew reached up where I was in the front seat and yanked me to the back. I was sent sprawling into Kate's and Chris' laps. He took my place in the front and fired a volley of shotgun blasts through the windshield sending the demonic creature flying backwards over the hood of the car. I felt the vibration run through the vehicle as we ran over the creature. Within seconds, we were in the garage, and the door was closing. I watched through the back window as the broken mass of the creature in the drive trembled and rose from the asphalt. The closing garage door obscured my view of the creature, but even as the door shut, I felt the impact of the creature as it hit against the garage door. Lionel quickly hit the remote to slam the metal doors into place, but I could still hear the angry shrieks coming from the creature.

Lionel, Matthew, and Christopher made a sweep of the house when we returned to make sure no welcoming party was lurking within the house. Lionel left Kate with me in the garage as they secured the house. When he was satisfied that no dark creatures were lurking hidden in the massive home, he came back for Kate and me.

"Go on in. It's clear. Masters Christopher and Matthew are going to help me drag the beast that managed to get in the house to the garage, and we'll burn it here. Get some sleep in Master Zell's room," Lionel ordered. "I'll show Miss Kate and Masters Christopher and Matthew to a bedroom to rest after we finish with the Dark One. We'll continue the search at first light."

"Thank you, Lionel," I whispered planting a light kiss on his cheek.

I took a long, hot, luxurious bath before putting on one of Zell's clean tee shirts. My dirty clothes had disappeared, and I was sure someone had taken them to wash.

I snuggled into Zell's bed. I loved it because I could smell the faint scent of him still on the sheets.

"I will find you tomorrow. I promise," I whispered into the dark and closed my eyes.

ꕥ8.THE SEARCH

DURING THE NIGHT I AWOKE TO THE SOUNDS OF howls, a sinister scraping sound something akin to nails scraping on a chalkboard and otherworldly screams. Getting up, I opened Zell's bedroom door and looked into the Great Room where a light was on. I could see Lionel sitting in an overstuffed leather chair in front of the fireplace with a rifle leaned against his knee. He had a pistol in his hand, which rested on the arm of the chair. Cautiously, I made my way toward him.

"Lionel?" I whispered.

"Yes, Miss Annie?" He answered back his voice barely above a whisper.

"What are those noises?" I asked in a shaky voice.

"Those," he replied, nodding toward the big screen. The cameras were fixed on the outside. I could not see anything but blackness. Abruptly, a crack of lightning and a boom of thunder sounded. In that brief moment when the sky was lit by the lightning, I could see the sinister winged creatures were still surrounding the house all standing looking toward it. Then, there were those creatures that were more frightening than any nightmare could conjure up. They were creeping and crawling about the yard, the drive, and the porch. Creatures with long, crooked nails were scraping them along the metal covers over the doors and windows. They were a countless number. As far as the camera could see, there were winged Dark Angels standing and gazing toward the house or Dark Ones crawling all over it.

"I thought there could only be one at a time," I said flatly.

"If they find a way in, hopefully, they will only send in one," Lionel answered never taking his eyes from the screen, "at a time," he added. I understood his meaning.

"Lionel did you see the Oprah show? There were two of them. Why?"

"Master Zell is also worried about that. Obviously, a couple of renegades are testing the boundaries. They don't like to play by the rules; however, the Archangels usually keep them in line."

"Those things out there look like angels. Are all those things fallen angels?" I asked Lionel.

"Yes, you know one third of an innumerable company of angels fell with Lucifer according to scripture," he answered solemnly.

"It looks as though they are all here. Are you afraid?" I asked Lionel.

Lionel turned his gaze from the screen and looked at me.

"What is there to fear?"

"Dying?" I countered.

"Annie, death is only a rebirth. If you've learned anything from Zell, it's that death is not the end of life. It's simply the beginning of another more beautiful existence. We must live to accomplish our mission in this life, but to die is gain. Death is nothing to fear. Be strong. Never be afraid to die for those things that are most sacred to you. We all have a destiny. Sometimes, that destiny is our death. Do you understand what I am saying?"

"I'm not sure."

"Just this. Never be afraid to die for what is right, for what is good. Sometimes, in our death glorious events happen: people change, nations change, faith is restored," Lionel finished.

"You sound like Zell." My eyes fell, and sadness settled over me. "Do you think Zell is OK?" I asked him.

"If anyone is strong enough to survive, it's Master Zell," Lionel said confidently. "He has a reason to fight and to live. You are his reason. He has resolutely waited throughout the ages for your coming. He will not be easily defeated. Come," Lionel said, standing and taking my hand, "you need to sleep."

I followed Lionel back to the bedroom suite. He walked to the bookcase and turned the stereo on playing some soothing music.

"This should help drown out the sounds of the night. Rest well, Miss Annie. I stand in Master Zell's place and will guard you with my life because you are sacred to him." With that, Lionel left the room. He was right. All I could hear was the soothing music. I lay back down, and soon I drifted off to sleep.

I woke to a light rapping on the bedroom door. Sleepily, I pulled the comforter back and set up on the side of the bed.

"Annie," I heard Kate call.

"Come in," I called out. Kate entered with my clothes that had disappeared from the room the evening before clean and folded. Her tattered clothing was replaced with jeans and a tee-shirt.

"Lionel has breakfast ready in the dining room. You should see it. There is food there I've never ever seen before. You better hurry because Christopher and Matthew are eating everything in sight."

"I am hungry. Our dinner last night was interrupted by *someone* banging on the door." I growled.

"Put these on, and I'll see you in the dining room," Kate laughed. "I'll try to save you some breakfast, but I may be in for a fight."

"Poor Matt and Chris, I've seen you fight," I replied waiting for Kate's reaction.

"Yeah, it's been a long time since I had that much fun," Kate chuckled. "Hurry up slow poke," she said as she disappeared from the room.

When I entered the dining room, I found Kate had not exaggerated. There was bacon, sausage, pork chops, small breakfast steaks, fried potatoes, eggs, hash brown casserole, a wide selection of fruit, sweet rolls, biscuits, toast, sliced tomatoes, gravy, hot and cold cereal, and an assortment of jellies. I put some fruit, bacon, hash brown casserole, and toast on my plate and sat down in the chair next to Kate. Immediately, a young lady put a glass of juice and a cup of coffee before me. I ate slowly watching Matt, Chris, Kate, and Lionel as Matt filled Lionel in on our efforts yesterday to find Zell.

"We'll take the Hummer. I already have it loaded with a small arsenal," Lionel offered. "As soon as we find Master Zell, you can take one of the vehicles from the garage while we have the rather gaping hole from Miss Annie's very effective shotgun blast repaired along with a new tailgate and paint job on your truck. Oh, I apologize for our chef's rather enthusiastic breakfast. We have never entertained company before. I think she was up all night in her excitement cooking for you."

I saw Matthew and Christopher look across the table at one another and grin like Cheshire Cats. They gave one another a high five. I met Lionel's gaze. He gave a slight shake of his head in disbelief, and I laughed out loud.

"We'll meet in the entry foyer in thirty minutes," Lionel said, rising and dismissing himself from the room.

"What happened last night at the boathouse?" Matthew asked fixing a curious stare on Kate and me.

"We fought a dark creature, and miraculously, we killed it. I followed Lionel's example and burned it just to make sure. Then you guys showed up. End of story," I smiled and shrugged my shoulders.

Matthew searched my face and looked at me suspiciously. His gaze traveled to Kate who gave him a fabulous smile and back to me. I could tell he didn't totally buy our story, but he let the subject drop.

An hour later, we were pulling off the interstate. Instead of searching the east side of Paces Ferry and finishing up the few streets we left uncovered, we all agreed to search the west side. Lionel suggested that I try to use the connection that Zell and I seemed to have to lead the search. He slowly drove through streets on the west side letting me lead by telling him to turn down this street then that. I asked Lionel to pull over after fifteen or twenty minutes of this. I threw open the door and stepped out into the fresh spring morning air. Closing my eyes, I inhaled deeply. I had to separate myself from the rest of the group and concentrate only on Zell. Standing very still and listening, I exhaled slowly. I began to walk hesitantly forward, eyes still closed, listening for the beat of Zell's eternal heart. I couldn't hear a heartbeat, but I thought I felt a pull to the right. I opened my eyes to get my bearings. I cut across a parking lot, then between two buildings. When I disappeared between the buildings, my friends in the car behind me went berserk. Chris and Matthew jumped from the vehicle and trailed me. Lionel and Kate backed up out of the parking lot to search for the place where I would emerge from the buildings. I crossed several yards, then across a street we had not been down. I hesitated closing my eyes once again and concentrating on Zell. The pull was unmistakable. I ducked between two rather large buildings into an alley and emerged in a common parking lot in the back. Backed up to a loading dock, the white van sat parked. I gasped for breath and backed up until I felt the solid bricks of a building in the alley pressed against my back. It actually worked. I think I may have found him. I used the building for support. I felt like I could swoon and faint at any moment. I waited until my erratic breathing slowed. My heart beat so violently against my chest that I was sure it could be heard for blocks.

I peered out around the corner of the building. No one was in sight only the van.

I jumped when I felt something touch my hand. It was Lionel.

"Oh, you scared me," I breathed heavily.

"I'm sorry, Miss Annie. Wait here," he told Matthew, Christopher and Kate. He nudged me around the corner. I was not sure if Lionel or Zell knew about Kate, but I did not feel comfortable telling anyone her secret. Silently, we moved toward the house. Lionel jumped up on a stoop to check the door. The door was locked. "How sure are you that Zell is in this building?"

"The feeling is strong," I whispered.

"Let's look for a way in that is quieter than knocking down this metal door," Lionel whispered back.

I followed Lionel, and he quietly checked the windows on the back of this building. A few feet from the loading dock were two basement windows. Lionel saw them about the same time that I did, and he moved toward them. He knelt down to look through the windows. He pushed against the first one, but it did not budge. He moved to the second window and pushed.

Groaning, it gave a few inches. Lionel grabbed a knife from his belt and slid it under the window moving it along the sill. A latch gave with a snap, and Lionel smiled.

"I'm going through here. Gather your friends and meet me by the back door. Hopefully, I'll let you in there. Give me fifteen minutes before you try to come in alone," Lionel ordered.

I nodded and gave him a hug. "Be careful."

"Always, Miss Annie," Lionel said smiling. "Always."

Although he must be mid to late forties, Lionel was very handsome. He had a smooth creamy complexion and dark hair that was always immaculately coiffed. Even in an adventure such as this, not a hair on his head was out of place. Large, dark eyes with long lashes filled his face. He had a nice mouth, not beautiful like Zell's, but nice. Lionel's powerfully built frame disappeared through the open window, and I stood to return to my friends.

"I think Zell is in this building. Lionel has gone to find us a way in," I whispered to Kate. We all crouched beside the large concrete stoop that was covered with a metal awning whose paint had virtually flaked off except for a stray fleck of dulled color here and there. I asked Matthew to tell me when fifteen minutes were up. I was anxious to get in the building and look for Zell. My stomach churned as though a virus had infiltrated it, but I knew its roots were my shattered nerves waiting for Lionel to come to the door.

"Time's up," Matthew whispered.

I took in a great gulp of air and rose. As if chained to me, everyone rose behind me. Ignoring the steps, I pulled myself up on the side of the crumbling concrete platform.

Kate took the steps. I noticed and gave her a knowing smile. If anyone didn't need the steps, it was Kate. Matthew and Chris followed me hoisting themselves up the side of the concrete stoop. I peered through the dirty window beside the door, but I didn't see Lionel or anyone else either. I tried the door again, but it was locked. Out of my peripheral vision, I saw movement to my right. I froze but managed to raise my right hand to halt my friend's movements. I turned. I saw the window to the basement raise, and an arm inched out waving. I motioned to Matt, Chris, and Kate to look toward the window. Their eyes widened, and they looked back to me in surprise. Was that Lionel's arm waving to us? I didn't know, but I moved to the edge of the stoop. Silently, I slipped from its side, and the others followed close behind me.

I stooped to peer into the darkness of the basement, but I could see nothing. Holding the window up, I slid the lower part of my body through. Then, I turned on my stomach and inched my way back through the window. Hanging my fingertips on the window sill, I dropped quietly to the floor. Temporarily, I was blinded as my eyes adjusted to the gloom of the basement. I could see a dark figure standing only a few feet from me.

"Lionel?" I questioned the dark shape.

"Yes, it's Lionel," whispered the dark shape. I wondered for a few moments if it really was Lionel as his voice was too low to be recognized. I reached out for him thinking if I touched this dark form that I would know if it was Lionel or a dark creature waiting for me. As I reached, the dark mass took my hand and stepped into the dim light which filtered through the dirty basement windows. It was Lionel. I felt as if the smile that stretched across my face would cover it entirely. I was never so glad to see anyone in my life.

"I am sorry that I could not get to the back door. There is a locked metal door at the end of the hall that leads to the back door with a guard sitting next to it. I felt this was the path of least resistance," Lionel whispered, trying to explain the need to enter this way.

A muffled expletive broke into our conversation. Christopher had caught his hand on a nail and ripped it open. Lionel opened a small leather pouch he wore belted around his waist. He withdrew a thin package and ripped it open. He poured it over the wound and covered it with a large bandage that he pulled from the same pouch. He shrugged his shoulders as I looked questionably at him.

"I did not know in what shape we might find Master Zell, so I brought a few things," he replied as if I had verbally asked him a question. "You will need to get a tetanus shot after we leave here unless you have had one recently," he whispered to Christopher. Finished with dressing Christopher's wound, he moved closer to us whispering. "There are a couple of guards and a couple of people in scrubs upstairs. I think Zell may well be in here. Why else would someone guard such a dilapidated building? The two in scrubs just left a room in the main hall. They may be taking a break. We need to move quickly. An intimidating chap, possibly a guard went in when they left. I have a plan," Lionel whispered, moving closer.

Upstairs, Lionel guided us to a room with a bed and a small dresser. On top of the dresser were several pairs of folded scrubs. Lionel closed the door silently behind us. Kate looked quickly through the scrubs and pulled out a top and bottom. While the others kept themselves occupied by looking into the hall through the few inches of space between the door and the door jam, I helped Kate into the scrubs.

"It certainly would help if you weren't so small," I commented gathering the loose folds of the scrubs.

"No problem. Zell's not the only one who can make himself larger you know," Kate said with a wink. Before my very eyes, Kate filled out to fit into the scrubs. "Better close your mouth before some insect that I know must be residing in this residence crawls in there." Kate giggled at the expression on my face. I still could not reconcile the fact that my childhood friend was a warrior angel—my guardian angel. This petite blonde has always watched my back since we were in pigtails and missing our front teeth. That thought stopped me cold. I don't remember Kate ever losing her front teeth. Why had that bizarre thought just now crossed my mind? Little unusual things from our childhood suddenly made sense. Kate never had zits, braces, or complained of menstrual cramps like the rest of my friends. Now, I was beginning to see what had eluded me before. Kate has never really been like the rest of us. She is an eternal being.

"Annie," Kate whispered a worried look on her face. "Are you OK?"

"Yeah," I growled playfully. "It's just beginning to become apparent why you never had zits."

Kate's hand flew to her mouth to stifle the laughter bubbling there, "You are too random, Annie," she choked out trying to be quiet. "I love you, you know. I don't think guardians are supposed to get involved with their wards, but you have always been my friend not just a human that I was assigned to protect." She abruptly hugged me, took my hand, and dragged me to the door where Lionel waited.

"I'm ready," she whispered. Matthew and Christopher looked bewildered and opened their mouths to say something, but closed them again. Wide-eyed they stared at Kate.

"Are you wearing your hair different today Kate?" Christopher asked.

"Yeah," Matthew whispered, "something's definitely different about you."

If Lionel noticed the difference in Kate, he didn't let on.

Kate made a face at Christopher and slipped out into the hall and knocked on the door of the room which Lionel had seen the guard enter. You could hear the lock snap and then the door creak as someone unseen opened the door. Kate stepped through without even looking our way. Only moments later the door opened again. Kate motioned to us. Soundlessly, we all made our way across the hall and into the room. Kate was closing a closet door on the guard who looked unconscious. His mouth, hands, and feet were bound with medical tape.

"How did you subdue him so quick," Matthew squeaked out trying to whisper.

"I didn't spend eight of the best years of my life in karate classes just for the black belt," she huffed dusting off her hands. Both Matthew and Christopher looked at her admiringly.

"My kind of woman," Matthew grunted. "You wanna try some moves on me when we get out of this mess?"

"Yeah, I'll move your nose around to your ear for you," Kate whispered back glaring at him.

"Oh yeah, baby. I love an aggressive woman," Matt growled.

Glancing in my direction, Kate rolled her eyes and laughed. A sound from the back of the room drew our attention back to the task at hand. Swiftly, I moved around a metal partition that had been erected separating the back of the room from the front. There on a bed lay Zell. A sob rose in my throat and escaped before I could stop it. I ran to his side and gathered him in my arms.

"I'm here, Zell. We've come to take you home," I whispered holding him tight. There was no response. Immediately, I checked his neck for a pulse. Sighing with relief, I felt the throb of a pulse. Carefully, I lowered him gently back on the bed while I assessed the situation. An IV needle was inserted in both arms. A bag of clear fluids was dripping into a vein on his left hand. The other arm also had a needle which led to a bag holding Zell's blood. They were draining him dry. Enraged, I reached for the bandage that held the needle in place on his right hand and slipped the needle from him. Lionel worked on the needle inserted into his left hand. Kate brought bandages to cover the wounds on both hands once we removed the needles.

Lionel once again reached into his black leather bag and removed a syringe.

"This is an antidote for the depressants that Zell has evidently been given to keep him sedated," Lionel explained as he gently inserted the needle into a vein in Zell's forearm and emptied it. "I anticipated something like this. Master Zell is much too strong to be imprisoned. I figured the only way someone could subdue him would be to heavily medicate him." He turned to Matthew and Christopher pulling out three pistols and handing them each one. He kept one for himself. "These are not the dark creatures we have faced before. These are humans. Those guns are tranquilizer guns. The pellets will down their targets in fifteen to twenty seconds. Let's go see that the rest of the vermin take a nice, long nap. Master Zell will have to go out through a door. We can't get him through the window in the basement."

A grin spread across Matt and Chris's face, "Let's do it," Matthew said sounding comical whispering the edict.

I returned to Zell's side and began to stroke his face. "Zell wake up. Zell, please," I whispered. "I kept my promise. I've come for you." Kate was rummaging through cabinets and drawers. "What are you doing?" I whispered.

"I'm looking for Zell's clothes," she answered. I left Zell's side to help her search. Kate stopped in her search lifting her head as if lost in thought. "Stay here," she ordered and left the room.

Moments later she reentered the room with a pair of scrubs from across the hall. "I think these will fit," she whispered. "Watch the hall. I'll get these on him."

I moved to the door and peeked out. There was no sign of Lionel, Matt, or Chris. Time seemed to stretch into an eternity. It seemed as though I had been standing there watching for hours when I knew it could have only been minutes. I heard a thud down the hall, then another. I held my breath wondering what I should do. I opened the door wider and stepped a foot into the hall. I would check out the sounds. Lionel, Matt, and Chris may be in trouble. I leaned against the door which I heard the sounds coming from and listened. I reached for the door knob and carefully, soundlessly turned it. An explosion sounded as the door flung open and a rather large man fell into my arms. I stumbled backward from the weight of him, and both of us fell onto the hard, dirty floor.

"Annie!" Matt cried.

"Get this guy off of me," my outrage was muffled by the bulk of him. He must have been the extra-large guy to whom the scrubs that Zell now wore belonged.

"Sorry, Annie. This guy took three of Lionel's tranquilizer pellets and still managed to get the door open." Christopher helped me up.

"Where is Lionel?" I asked dusting myself off.

"He's checking out the rest of the building," replied Chris.

The three of us entered the room to find Zell dressed in the bottom half of the scrubs but still unconscious. Running to him, I put my arms around him.

"We've come to take you home," I whispered.

"Look at this!" Kate cried, throwing open a small refrigerator in the room. There were bags of blood, Zell's blood, stored in an open container. No wonder he was so weak. I was furious.

"Who would do . . . ," I began. The door crashed open and all four of us, Kate, Matthew, Christopher, and myself moved around the partition. A man stood in the doorway. I recognized the man as one of the doctors from my hospital room. Not Dr. Patel, but one of the doctors who was present during my transfusion. I remembered him because I remembered his eyes. All the other doctors had warm eyes. This doctor had cold eyes—eyes of the dead, staring but not seeing eyes. He came in many times while I was recovering to check on me. Now, I suspected spying on me was what he was really doing. I remember I always wondered why he came in. I thought he came because he was curious. He just came to see if I made it through another night. His eyes told me that he didn't really care whether I lived or died. Now, he was here. It was becoming obvious that he had something to do with Zell's disappearance.

Hate rose in my throat like vomit. I forced it back down. Why was he doing this to Zell? Then, knowing fell around me like a misty cloak. He wanted Zell's blood. He saw how I recovered after the transfusion from Zell, and he wanted his blood. I found my voice.

"You're a doctor from the hospital," I stated simply.

"Yes, how bright you are," he sneered, "too bad for you." He pulled a gun from his coat pocket and pointed it at me. Matthew and Christopher started for him, and he turned the gun toward them aiming first at one, then the other. I put my hands out to stop them.

"Wait," I raised my voice. "Did you do this to Zell?" I asked the doctor.

"You don't think those idiots lying unconscious in the other room planned this, do you?"

"But why?" I asked even though I thought I knew the answer to the question.

"Your friend's blood has some interesting qualities, and I have a son dying from leukemia," he answered motioning to Zell with the gun.

"Why didn't you just ask Zell to help you?"

"Why would he help me or my son?" The doctor sneered.

"Because he is good," I replied simply.

"Humph," the doctor sneered. "Once his blood has healed my son, I am going to become rich healing the wealthy. Your friend is my private manufacturing plant."

I gasped. "You can't be serious. You are a doctor. How could you do that to another human being?"

"I don't think he is a human being," the doctor snarled. "No human that I've ever seen has blood that will heal." Matthew and Christopher looked first at me, and then they looked at Zell. "Too bad you have dragged your friends into this," he stated coldly pointing the gun at Matthew.

"No, too bad your heart is so black," Lionel replied coolly from behind the doctor. Lionel slipped silently up behind him and stuck his tranquilizer gun to his back. Of course, the doctor didn't know it was only a tranquilizer gun and raised his hands slowly. Christopher stepped forward and wrenched the gun from the doctor's hands.

"Please," the doctor's voice turn from sinister to pleading. "Please, I only took him to heal my son."

"We might have believed that earlier before your frank confession of greed once your son is healed," I retorted.

"Please," the doctor begged. I looked at him. His eyes were still cold, but were mine?

I made a decision and walked quickly to the cabinet beside the refrigerator filled with Zell's blood. I took a syringe out of the box and popped the cap from over the needle. Opening the refrigerator, I took out a bag of blood and inserted the needle into the port in the side of the bag. I withdrew a syringe full of Zell's blood and placed the cap back over the needle. I walked back to the doctor and held out the syringe.

"For your son," I offered. With a shaking hand, the doctor took the syringe. "I've decided not to call the police just yet. Perhaps, we can take this evil that you have perpetrated on our friend and the planned evil you had in mind for us and turn it into some good. How about you open your office for the poor two days a month, visits and treatment completely free of charge? What do you say?"

"You would trust this guy?" Matthew asked incredulously.

"Absolutely not! Kate, take out your cell and take photos of this whole setup, the doctor here, the goons passed out in the other room, and of course the crime vehicle, the van." Kate giggled and immediately began snapping pictures.

"Also," I added. "I'll be in touch with your office. I'd like to volunteer my help on those days. We'll become great friends, I'm sure. I volunteered at Doc Newcomb's Veterinary Hospital the last two summers. In fact, Doc

Newcomb taught me how to use a needle. She'll be delighted that I'm helping out the good doc here now." I grinned enjoying the doctor's immense discomfort. "For good measure Kate, get Dr. . . ." I looked at the doctor waiting for a response.

"T . . . T . . . Tapp," Dr. Tapp stammered.

"Kate, get Dr. Tapp's confession on your cell's voice recorder too before we leave here." I took the syringe filled with Zell's blood back out of the doctor's hands. "In fact, we'll just hold on to this syringe until Kate gets an acceptable confession. Shoot him Lionel if he doesn't cooperate," I smiled at Lionel knowing full well he held only a tranquilizer pistol on the doctor. I was beginning to enjoy this. I walked to the refrigerator and put the top on the cooler full of bags of Zell's blood. I found a bag in the drawer and filled it with a box of syringes that were in the cabinets. I had an idea. If Zell agreed, I would have a use for his blood.

Kate put her phone on record and stuck it in the doctor's face. "Start blabbing," she ordered.

"On May 5th I hired four men to kidnap Mr. Zell Starr. My purpose for the kidnapping was to save the life of my son using the healing properties that his blood seems to have," the doctor stopped. Lionel gouged him with the gun.

"Keep talking," Lionel growled.

"I planned to keep Mr. Starr indefinitely using him as my private blood bank. I planned to make millions from wealthy patients using his blood to heal their terminal illnesses. My name is Dr. John Tapp, and this is my confession to the crime of kidnapping Mr. Zell Starr." Dr. Tapp finished and hung his head.

I handed the cooler and a bag of syringes to Matthew and Christopher.

"Do you guys know where the Hummer is parked?" I asked them.

"Yeah, just around the corner," Christopher answered.

"Bring it to the back door. Kate and I will try to wake Zell. Lionel can escort Dr. Tapp to his vehicle," I sighed, suddenly tired. Lionel motioned for the doctor to move.

"I'll see you in a few weeks," I said cheerfully to Dr. Tapp. "Oh, and all this is our little secret. No talking to anyone about Zell, or we all do some talking—to the cops." I turned my back to him and touched Zell's cheek. "Wake up, Zell," I whispered in his ear. Nothing. He didn't bat an eyelash. I looked at Kate with tears in my eyes. "Is he going to be OK? The doctor took a lot of blood in a short amount of time."

"He'll be fine," Kate assured me moving to my side to hug me.

"Is that the eternal, all-knowing being speaking or my human best-friend Kate?" I asked, searching her face.

"I'm not all-knowing Annie, but I believe Zell will pull through this. He is one tough cookie; you know," Kate whispered gently looking around the room to make sure we were alone.

"Yes, I know," I whispered leaning over and burying my face in his neck to hide the tears that were flowing down my cheeks.

"Zell, please open your eyes—please," I sobbed my heart breaking.

"Annie," Lionel ordered returning to the room. "Speak those things that are not as though they are," Lionel said gently.

I was confused by what he said. Speak those things that are not as though they are? I thought about what he was trying to convey to me.

"What you are saying is . . . ," I stopped examining his words in my head. "That I should speak as though Zell was healthy and recovered?" I asked.

"Speak it into being," Lionel spoke softly.

"I don't know how," I murmured.

"Yes, you do," he answered soothingly.

"Lionel, Zell will open his eyes in a moment, and we'll go home," I spoke my longings aloud.

"Yes, that's it, Miss Annie," Lionel encouraged.

"Zell is alive. He is healthy and strong," I said a little more convincingly, and Lionel smiled.

"Zell is opening his eyes," I looked at Zell's still face. "Zell is strong and well," I said again. "Zell, open your eyes, baby," I almost sobbed. Amazed, I thought I saw his dark eyelashes flutter. "Zell!" I shouted out loud. "Open your eyes!" Slowly, his eyes flickered open for a moment then closed again. "Zell, your strength is back. Open your eyes."

"Is that you making all that racket, Annie?" Zell asked weakly still not opening his eyes.

"Yes, yes, it's me," I sobbed throwing my arms around him.

"I want to leave this place, Zell. Open your eyes, get up, and let's go."

Zell smiled and very slowly opened his eyes scrunching them up as though the light filtering through the windows was hurting his eyes.

"I'll be your huckleberry. I'll get you out of here," he said still not moving.

"Well, you're cute and all, but you're not Doc Holiday," I replied. Zell was coming back. He was repeating my favorite movie line to me from the movie, "Tombstone." "I would elope with Doc Holiday," I said teasing him.

Finally, Zell opened his eyes and raised himself up on his elbows. "How about me?" he asked slightly swaying. "Would you elope with me?" Our eyes locked. I was not sure whether he was being silly or serious. Regardless, I had only one answer.

"You should be so lucky," I teased. Zell laughed weakly.

༄9. THE HEALING

BACK AT HIS LAKE HOUSE ZELL IMPROVED
remarkably. Though still weak, he talked, joked with me,
and ate like a horse. I called Dad to tell him the good
news, and to ask if I could stay in Zell's guest room
through the night. Zell would have it no other way. If I
left, he was going also, and he really needed to regain his
strength before fighting any Dark Creatures. We were
safe in his fortress home.

That evening Zell and I ate homemade soup and
sandwiches on the sofa before a great fire in the fireplace.
Lionel lowered the metal doors and shutters because Zell
was too weak to do much fighting. Lionel insisted on the
fire to keep the Dark Ones at bay and turned on the air
conditioning since it was the first of May. I could not take
my eyes from Zell. I was so happy to have him back. I
fluffed up his pillows. I dabbed at the corners of his
mouth with a napkin.

"All this attention is a little disconcerting, Annie,"
Zell complained good-naturedly.

"I've missed you," I said shyly.

"May I record that?" Zell asked. "A couple of
months ago you were calling me a stalker."

"I've changed my mind," I whispered.

"What does your mind tell you about me now?" He
asked.

"That you're my friend," I whispered again, but I looked him straight in his silver eyes.

"Is that all? Just your friend?" He asked.

"My best friend," I answered.

"Kate's your best friend," he retorted.

"Kate is my best female friend," I countered. "You're my best male friend."

"That's not enough Annie."

"Why?" I asked.

"I want to be more," Zell leaned in close.

"I'm not sure how much more I can give right now."

"Will you be my girl?" Zell whispered while dragging his lips across mine but not quite kissing me.

"Your girl?" I repeated.

"Yes, my forever girl."

"What is a forever girl?" I murmured against his lips.

"A promise to be my girl until the day I die," he ran his lips just beneath my chin making me shiver.

"What if I die first?" I asked.

"The day you die *is* the day I die," he kissed the spot on my face just before my ear.

"Is that a premonition?" I asked a little unnerved. I was not sure whether his statement unnerved me or the attention he was giving me unnerved me.

"No, it's not a premonition just a promise. I'll never live another day without you." Zell answered quietly sitting back. "All the thousands of years I have lived, I would give for one more day with you. I have never lived until you were born merely existed."

"Don't talk like that, it frightens me," I whispered. "Did you never have a girlfriend Zell? A sweetheart?"

"I had my first vision of you at age fourteen. After that, every girl I looked upon, I thought of you. I even compared her to you. No other ever had a chance for my heart. It had already been given away," he looked at me so intensely that my breath caught in my throat.

"How sad that you waited thousands of years for me. Were you lonely?" I asked.

"Terribly lonely at times, but I had plenty of battles to fight. I always knew you were out there waiting in the future for me," he whispered.

"Why did you wait so long to make yourself known to me?"

"It's hard to explain. I waited for you so long that I was afraid. I guess I was afraid you would reject me. Which you did," he laughed. "Then, I thought I had waited too long; Jon became your boyfriend. I resigned myself to the fact that I was going to have to love you from afar. That we probably never would meet. That I was only going to be your protector and nothing else," Zell looked away. That hurt faraway look had returned to his eyes. "Do you know what it was like to watch you kiss someone else?"

"I can imagine," I replied, thinking back to the times that I had thought that there had been others before me and the pain that I felt. "You just said that you love me."

"Yes, I love you. I've finally found my home in you, Annie. I will love you forever. The question is Annie, do you love me?" Zell turned and met my eyes.

"I . . . I . . . I . . .," I stammered. I knew I did. I wanted to grab him and scream, "Yes, I love you more than life itself." But I couldn't, and I didn't know why.

Zell pushed himself up and rose from the sofa.

"Good night Annie," he whispered, turned, and left the room. I could see the lost look in his eyes. I could see the pain.

What was the matter with me? Why couldn't I open up to him? Why couldn't I tell him about my feelings? I know when my mother died, I just stopped feeling or believing in anything. It was easier that way. No love, no pain. No love, no loss. I've lived without my mother for thirteen years, and it has left me empty. I tried not to feel anything for Zell. I tried. I fought the waves of feelings, and I lost. I am inescapably, inexorably in love with Zâzêl Starr, The Last of the Anak. His presence filled my every waking moment, and dreams of him pervaded my nights. Now, I have hurt him. If I knew how that moment of my silence would affect future events, I would run to him, throw myself in his arms, and confess my feelings for him. If, I knew.

The next morning Zell brought breakfast to the guest room where I slept. "Eat something. Afterwards, we'll go by your house for you to dress for school. I know you don't want to wear those clothes for the third day in a row."

"Are you sure you feel up to school?" I grabbed a muffin and a cup of coffee.

"Yes."

"Just yes?"

"Yes."

"OK. I'll be ready in ten minutes," I said carrying the muffin and coffee into the adjoining bath.

A shower and a fresh change of clothes did wonders for my mood. I excitedly talked about graduation which was only a week away. I was also excited about our plans for tonight, but Zell was quiet and looked worried.

"What's bothering you?" I asked him.

"Something could go wrong. You could get hurt,".

"You worry too much," I laughed. "If we stick to the plan, nothing will go wrong."

"I don't guess that I can change your mind about this," he answered.

"If you don't feel well enough for this adventure, we won't go. If you just don't want to go through with it, we won't," I replied. Zell looked at me and grimaced.

"I think it is a great plan, but my life has been devoted to protecting you. This is an unnecessary risk."

"We could at least try it. If we encounter any problems, we'll stop and return home. I promise that I will not argue if you want to stop."

Zell sighed, "It's a date then."

"Date," I agreed and gave him a quick hug.

The school day dragged by. I looked at my watch every few minutes. We were reviewing for final exams, and if that wasn't boring enough, tonight's plan constantly played over and over in my head. I looked for flaws in our plans. I imagined a thousand ways our plan could go wrong and fail. I was exhausted by the end of the school day.

Zell was quiet all day. Maybe, he didn't feel well and was hiding it from me. He could be worried about tonight, or he may still be hurt from my lack of commitment last night. I added Zell to my list of things to worry about. Finally, the last bell rang, and I gathered my books. He was standing next to me when I finally dragged myself from the desk chair. We walked in silence to his car.

"Zell, about last night, I want to explain . . . ," I began.

"Don't Annie, I don't think I can talk about it," Zell remarked looking straight ahead.

"But, I want to explain . . . ," I began again.

"Let's talk about it later. I can only think about this crazy plan of yours today," Zell sighed. I stopped trying to talk to him. I didn't want him to change his mind about tonight.

As soon as school was out, we headed for Zell's house on the lake. We packed Zell's blood in a soft pack cooler, and he brought along a duffel bag with his Anak apparel.

"Are you absolutely sure you want to do this?" Zell asked me as we stepped out into the warm evening air.

"Absolutely," I replied, putting first one arm then the other around his neck.

Zell gathered me in his arms and held me tight. He looked into my eyes with such love that I wanted to blurt out my feelings for him. I lowered my gaze instead. I felt him sigh, and his beautiful wings slowly unfolded and reached heavenward. Within moments, we were airborne. The sun was setting on the horizon when we landed. I reached into the cooler and withdrew the syringe that I had prepared before we left. I hid the cooler in some shrubbery close by.

We walked through the doors of Saint Jude's Research Hospital, and Zell walked me to a waiting room. "I can move fast enough that I most likely will never be noticed," he explained. He sat me on a chair and squatted before me. "Annie, this is a noble plan of yours. Don't think that I don't want to do this. I just don't like leaving you for even a few minutes."

"I'll be right here when you get back. I don't like it when you leave me either," I whispered stroking the sides of his face. "I have the letter ready. Please choose the sickest child here," I pleaded.

Zell caressed my cheek, then turned and walked down the hall. I watched him as he entered the elevator.

Twenty minutes later, Zell walked out of the elevator smiling. I waited serenely for him in the waiting room. "Part one of Annie's Plans complete," he said smiling.

"Have you found a child? Whom did you choose?" I asked, whispering even though I don't know why I whispered. The waiting room was empty.

"A little seven year old boy named Branson. I overheard the nurses say that he would not live through the night. His parents are in there which complicates the plan somewhat. I will need you to create a distraction."

"I have a better idea. Can you get me some nurse's scrubs?"

"Yes, I think so. Wait here. I'll see what I can find."

Ten minutes later, Zell returned with a bulge under his shirt. I laughed as he pulled a set of blue scrubs, a blue cap and mask from underneath his shirt.

"I expect you'll be pulling a rabbit out from under that shirt next. Hold on. I'll be right back," I called over my shoulder as I slipped into a restroom across from the elevator doors.

Minutes later, I opened the door and poked my head out making sure no one but Zell was in my line of vision.

"Here put these clothes in your bag," I ordered and held out a wad of clothing that I just came out of. We hid his bag behind an enormous plant in the lobby. "Take me to Branson."

We rode the elevator up to the third floor. I pulled my hair back in a ponytail, and on the ride up, I shared my plan with Zell. At the end of the corridor, we slowed. We peeked around the corner, and Zell pointed out Branson's room.

"Give me five minutes," I whispered to Zell.

Cautiously, I opened the door to Branson's room. The scene inside the room made me want to weep. A man and a woman, I assume Branson's parents, sat in chairs pulled as close to the bed as possible. They each held one of his tiny hands sandwiched between theirs. The woman's tears splashed on the sheets making an ever increasing wet spot there. The man's head was bowed resting against his son's tiny legs. I could hear Branson's labored breath. He appeared unconscious.

"Mr. and Mrs. Bowman may I speak to you for a moment?" I asked, standing in the doorway.

"Yes, of course," Mrs. Bowman answered as Mr. Bowman stood to greet me.

"If you don't mind, may we step out in the hall so that we could speak without disturbing Branson?"

"If we will only be a few minutes," Branson's dad replied. "They don't expect him to . . . they don't expect it to be much longer," he finished as if his heart was breaking.

"I know that is why it is imperative that I speak to you both."

The Bowmans followed me out into the hall. I walked about fifteen feet from the door and turned. I positioned myself so that in order to talk to me, the Bowman's backs would be to the door. No sooner than I began speaking, I saw Zell in his silver and gold armor walk silently into Branson's room.

"Mr. and Mrs. Bowman, we have an experimental procedure that has just come into our possession. We believe that this procedure will heal your son. I would like your permission to commence this procedure immediately. It has been used in another case recently where the recipient was minutes from death. Within a week, that recipient was healed and back at school. Trust me when I say, I believe without a shadow of a doubt that your son also will have favorable results. It only takes a few moments. May we begin?"

Branson's parents both inhaled deeply.

"What is this? Why are we just now hearing about it?"

"Until very recently, this procedure was unavailable. If I am to proceed, I must begin now. Do I have your permission to give your son an injection? That is all it is—an injection. He should begin to respond almost immediately. May I start now?"

"Yes, of course," Branson's father injected. "We are all out of options. Branson has been in a coma for the last three days. We have been told he will not survive the night."

"Wait here momentarily. I will be right back," I hurried into Branson's room and found Zell standing by Branson's bed.

"What did his parents say?" Zell asked when I entered the room.

"They gave their permission."

"Wonderful. I'll only be a few minutes."

Silently, I slipped back into the hall.

"It's done," I told his parents.

"Already?"

"Yes."

"Thank you," his parents hugged me briefly. "May we go back in?"

"Of course." I responded. "May I request something in return?"

"Yes," Branson's parents looked at one another confused.

"Raise him as a child of faith. He is now a flesh and blood miracle."

"Certainly," Branson's mother answered looking at her husband as if daring him to argue, and they headed to their son's room.

I heard a low squeal as I followed Branson's parents back into the room. I peered around them, and I saw what caused Branson's mother's consternation. Zell had not left the room yet. He stood magnificently in the corner in his armor. His hair blew gently around his face. He was as tall as the room would allow at about eight feet.

"Fear not," he said gently. "I bring you good tidings. Your son will live. Give thanks unto the Almighty."

Branson's mother sank to the floor sobbing beside his bed. Zell moved to her, and he gently lifted her to her feet. His alabaster face was shining and a halo enveloped his whole body.

"Woman, do not despair. Your son is healed."

"Mommy, Daddy," little Branson cried out as he opened his eyes and saw his parents. "An angel came and made me better."

"Sweetheart," Branson's mother wept as she gathered him in her arms. Branson's father wrapped his arms around them both.

Zell and I quietly left the room.

"What happened?" I whispered.

"He woke up before I even finished the injection. The little fellow didn't even whimper," Zell eyes began to cloud over as he relayed his story. "Branson thought I was an angel come to take him to heaven. I told him God was not taking him tonight that I had brought him medicine to make him well. I told him he was going home with his mother and father very, very soon. I was not too sure about your plan Annie, but when I looked into the eyes of that sick child, I knew you were right. I believe now that this is the best possible outcome for Dr. Tapp's evil plans. These children are so sick that it breaks my heart.

"Let's go to Plan Two. We have to get back. We have exams tomorrow," I half cried and half laughed as I pulled the letter out of my pocket. I wiped my tears off the letter as I seemed unable to stop crying.

Hastily, I wrote in Branson's name in the space that I had left for it in the letter.

Dear Doctors,

    This cooler contains a rare and unusual blood that has unique healing qualities. This blood is compatible with any blood type. We have injected one of your children, Branson Bowman, with his parent's permission, with this miraculous blood. Instead of dying tonight, he should make a complete recovery. It doesn't take much. Only a half of a syringe should do. Please perform any tests necessary to prove the validity of our claim, but trust us, it will heal any child in this hospital. Our only request is that you heal as many children as possible.

    Your friends and benefactors,

    A and Z

"Hopefully, the hospital staff will take this seriously, especially now that Branson will recover and live."

"I think I'll deliver this as the Annunaki. That should get their attention and make their night," Zell whispered conspiratorially. I was exhilarated that he was getting into the spirit of giving his gift.

"Yes, do," I whispered back excitedly clapping my hands. Zell paused to wink at me and then disappeared to retrieve the cooler. Only a couple of minutes later, I saw him come around the corner headed in the direction of the nurse's station where a half-dozen nurses milled about. I followed behind at a distance. The look on the face of each nurse was priceless as they saw this glowing warrior stride purposefully down the hall.

"Who is the supervising nurse or doctor on duty tonight?" His voice boomed.

"I am," a silver-haired nurse answered and stepped forward. All the nurses at the station froze and stopped what they were doing. A look of terror was written on their faces.

"Fear not. I have not come to do harm, but to share a great gift," Zell said gently. "In this cooler is a miracle. It should heal every terminally ill child that you have here. I have administered it to Branson Bowman already. He will not die tonight. He will live. Please read the enclosed letter as it will explain what you need to know. Have a pleasant evening," Zell offered, smiling brilliantly as he turned to go.

"Who are you?" The head nurse asked.

"I am Zâzêl, the last of the Annunaki, and the answer to these children's prayers." With that Zell turned and strode away, resplendent in his armor. I stood down the hall and watched as he walked briskly toward me. He grabbed my hand, and we headed for the stairwell. As soon as we hit the fresh air, Zell turned, took me in his arms, and left the ground simultaneously. He kissed me often on the return trip home. I think his generous gift had lifted the gloom that I had caused the previous evening. His kisses still made me a mess even though the effects were not as severe as in the beginning when we kissed. His kisses did make me relax, and I returned his kisses passionately.

Zell had me home by nine o'clock. He opened the door for me and saw me safely inside.

"You were right Annie. We did a very good deed tonight. Rest well love," he whispered as he kissed my cheek. Then, he turned and left.

❧10.AZAZELL

"WHY ARE YOU HERE?" I HEARD ZELL ROAR.

"I've come for her," the unknown voice replied.

"That will never happen," I could hear the strain in Zell's voice.

"It must, my son," the voice said sternly.

"Not as long as there is breath in my body," I could hear the anger in Zell's voice.

"She has to die," the voice said sadly.

"Not on my watch," Zell replied.

The voice laughed, "Cute little play on words, son of Watcher."

"She is mine," Zell ground out the words.

"You can't have her. She is too big a threat to our kind," the voice turned glacial.

"Your kind father, not my kind," Zell's voice became icy too.

Was this being that stood before me talking about me as though I wasn't there Zell's father? Zell is a striking figure in his Anak transformation, but this man that stood opposite Zell was absolutely terrifying. He was a few inches taller than Zell, and his hair was blacker than a moonless night. His features were as beautiful as Zell's, but his eyes and expression were cold. He was magnificent, although in a frightening way. I could see Zell's face in his just without the warmth and humanity that Zell's face possessed.

"You can't stop me," the voice argued.

"I'll die trying, father," Zell stated coldly.

"I don't want you to die, son. You're the only good that has ever come out of my existence."

"Then leave us," Zell ordered.

"For now, son. Only for now," Azâzêl whispered as he turned and left walking through the wall as if it didn't exist.

The sun came through my window waking me from a troubled sleep. The first thing that I wondered was if the conversation from last night was a dream or if a reality. Had Zell's father come last night to kill me, and Zell intervened?

Final exams began today. Since Zell and I missed several days when I was in the hospital, in Chicago, and New York, we were not exempt from our exams. The good news was that we only had to stay for exams, and then we were free for the rest of the day. Yesterday, someone called from the CNN network wanting to schedule an interview and film parts of my graduation for a human interest story. The interview was this afternoon. Then, Zell and I would study for the two exams scheduled for tomorrow. After that, my senior year was over except for the graduation ceremony on Saturday. The thought was both sad and exciting. I was closing one chapter of my life and beginning another. I wondered what my future held. Do I even have a future? Would there be a Dark Creature that Zell could not defeat? Would one of those deadly creatures find me without Zell one day? I sighed. I was unusually anxious today. I wondered at the cause of my anxiety. Was it finals that upset me? Was it the interview? Was it the dream last night or the possibility that it was real? Is Zell's father going to try to kill me? Or, could it be the uncertainty of my future? Perhaps, it was all of it.

⟲11.NEW BEGINNINGS

SATURDAY MORNING WAS BEAUTIFUL. AN AZURE sky promised that graduation would be an event worth remembering. Butterflies in my stomach seemed to want their freedom as they tumbled around in my stomach. A film crew was already outside ready to film me as I left for the graduation ceremony. I moaned as I opened the door and saw them leaned up against their vans taking a smoke break. Quickly, I closed the door before they saw me. I leaned against the door, sighing. I wondered where Zell was. I knew he was somewhere close just waiting to make an appearance at a suitable hour.

"Is there a problem?" Dad asked, walking into the room.

"Yes," I answered, "The paparazzi have arrived," I groaned.

Dad laughed, "Fame does seem to have a price."

"A high price," I smiled. Dad was such a good father, and I so loved him. I felt a pang of guilt that I had deprived him of his wife for so many years. A wife he obviously adored. If what Zell said is true, and I had no reason to doubt him, my mother was not killed in the accident but trying to save me. Sadness descended upon me like a cloud. I had to shake myself out of my gloomy mood. This was to be a day of happiness, a momentous day, a rite of passage, the day when I changed status from that of a schoolgirl to a young woman. I moved to hug my father.

"I love you, Dad," I murmured as I hugged him.

"I loved you first, baby," Dad choked as he said the words and held me to him.

"I love you more," I whispered. For as long as I can remember, we have repeated the same words almost every time one of us told the other that they were loved.

"Come in the kitchen. I've made breakfast. We'll eat, and then get ready for the graduation ceremony." Dad put his arm around me, and we walked into the kitchen.

"Zell came by my office yesterday to ask if he could take us to dinner after the graduation ceremony," Dad shared as we ate our breakfast of toast, bacon, and scrambled eggs.

"What did you tell him?" I asked.

"I told him that I would really like that, but I would have to check with you,"

"I don't have any plans until this evening. Zell and I have been invited to a party," I replied.

"How do you feel about Zell?" Dad asked suddenly getting serious.

"I like him Dad," I answered cringing at having this very personal conversation with my father. I needed my mother, a sister, or even Kate at a time like this.

"Is that all? You only like him?" He looked very serious."

"Dad, we're just friends," I said in an exasperated tone.

"I don't think Zell thinks you're merely friends," Dad remarked.

"Why do you say that?" I asked.

"Zell told me of his feelings for you yesterday also. You're it for him, Annie,"

"What do you mean?" I asked flustered.

"I just mean that I think his feelings for you seem to be real. I don't think there will ever be another girl that captures Zell's heart. Annie, I know who Zell is. He revealed himself to me in the hospital. He was frightening, beyond frightening, but it was the only way he could convince me to allow the transfusion. I've seen him before when you were just a little girl. I thought he was an angel. Perhaps, he still is an angel to me. He has evidently saved your life many times, and for that I will be eternally grateful to him. You're my baby, Annie. As long as Zell is in your life, I can rest a little easier. Things like this are difficult to speak about. It's times like this that I wish your mother were here.

"Me too," I whispered.

Dad sighed, but continued, "It's just every time I see you, every time I hug you, every time I turn out your light at night, I'm afraid it will be the last time. If what Zell says is true, you have a heavy burden to carry sweetheart."

"It has to be a true, Dad; otherwise, these evil, horrible creatures would not be trying to kill me."

My father closed his eyes as if in pain, and nodded his head. "I wish this burden could be lifted from you."

"Sometimes I do too, Dad, but then at times, I'm ready for the fight. I'm ready to do what I can to make the world a better place. Perhaps in a way, I too, am the last, the last hope for the redemption of mankind, the last person that will have the power to persuade people to take a stand for what is right and good in this world."

My father reached over and covered my hand with his. "You have been such a joy in my life. I can't bear the thought that I may lose you."

"Whatever happens, Dad, it is my destiny. It is the reason I was born. I believe Zell is right. This path that I have been pushed down rather unwillingly is my destiny. You know mother's death was my fault. I owe my mother this much. I owe it to her to make my life count for something, so she did not die in vain."

"Whatever are you talking about Annie? Your mother died in a car accident, and you were only a baby." Dad looked puzzled even as a small sob-like sound slipped out.

"There was a Dark One in the car that day of the accident. It was trying to get to me. Mother fought him, and he killed her. She was not killed in the accident. She was already dead. Zell was there. He tried to save us both."

Emotions washed over my father in waves. At first, I could see the shock in his eyes, then shock turned to anger. Finally, sadness settled back into them, and I had to look away.

"I'm sorry dad," tears began to fill my eyes, spill over, and run down my cheeks.

My father came around the table and put his arms around me. "It's not your fault. Don't you ever think that it is. There has to be a reason for all this."

"Zell was there that day. Mother just didn't crash. One of those creatures was trying to kill me. Mother fought him. She wouldn't let the creature have me. It attacked her, and she crashed the car. Zell had to make a decision to save me or mother. He chose me, but I wish he hadn't. I wish he had saved my mother."

"Annie, there's no use dwelling on the accident. What's done is done. For a long time, I was almost unbearably sad, but I believe I will see your mother again. I only have to wait. Though, I'll never have to wait as long as Zell has waited for you. Somehow, knowing he survived the agony of waiting for you, his true love, has given me hope and strength. While I am a mere mortal, if he can endure thousands of years waiting for his love, I can surely endure a few decades. Who could blame him for choosing to save you? You are the love of his life," Dad whispered covering my hand with his own.

"Don't say that Dad," I cried. "There's something else too."

"What dear?"

"I saw her."

"Saw who?"

"Mom, I saw her."

"You saw your mother?"

"Yes, when I died. I was in the hospital. I left my body, and she was there waiting for me."

"Are you sure you were not dreaming, Annie?"

"I'm positive. At first, you were at home talking to Larry, the deacon of your church. I could see you. I could see Zell flying to the hospital with me in his arms. Then I remember seeing myself in the emergency room. You and Zell were in the waiting room. You were praying. Zell was gazing out of the window. Then the next thing I know, I'm in an operating room, and I see Zell lying on a table. Suddenly, I'm in a beautiful place, and mother is walking toward me. I've been trying to find the right time to tell you because she sent you a message."

"A message?" Dad's voice sounded broken.

"Yes, she said to tell you that she loves you so much. She said love is eternal. Love survives death. She took me to a beautiful place much like Zell's island, and she waits for us there. She is with us too. Every time we think of her, she is near. She told me that I had to come back. This work that I am doing is my destiny. She affirmed that. She says that I will refocus the world on beauty and righteousness."

Dad's head dropped, and I could see the tears splashing on the table as they dropped from his eyes.

Sherry Fortner

"You were right, Dad. There is a God who loves us and has a plan for us. I was wrong to blame him for my mother's death. I was wrong not to have faith."

I held my father in my arms as he sobbed as if his heart was breaking all over again. After a while, he stopped. He looked at me and smiled through his tears.

"We'll let the subject drop for now, dear," Dad said gathering me in his arms and kissing the top of my head. "Thank you for sharing your mother's message with me. I knew that I would see her again. I am so happy that you were able to talk to her and hold her again. I'm sure she will be with us today at your graduation. Go and get ready. Today is supposed to be a happy day—not one of tears. You have a high school to graduate from today, and you've a new life to begin."

꧁12.GRADUATION

I DID NOT CONSIDER MYSELF MUCH OF A
material girl, but I did love clothes, shoes, and riding to
graduation with my father and Zell in his convertible.
The parking lot was chaos. The news crews were there
camera ready. The local stations had picked up on the
national network being there, and the three local stations
were camped out by the entrance too. Evidently, they
didn't want to be caught unaware if something did
happen during the graduation ceremony. All the local
politicians were there too. I guess they needed the free
publicity. One of them, the mayor, had several cameras
fixed on him as he spoke of this momentous day as
though someone had found a cure for cancer instead of it
being merely a high school graduation. Zell and I looked
at one another and exchanged a smile. Zell and my father
were in the front seat. Dad and Zell opened their doors
and climbed out. Then, Zell leaned over and scooped me
out of the back seat. Surprised, I locked my arms around
his neck.

"I'll have to make you ride in the back seat more
often," he teased whispering in my ear.

"Put me down you big oaf," I growled.

Zell laughed and hugged me tight. He kissed me on
the neck below my ear while he held me in his arms. My
heart stopped beating for a long second. I liked that
much more than I wanted to admit. I smacked him

playfully with my graduation cap that I held in my hand, and reluctantly, he placed me on the ground.

"I'm going on in and get a seat since you two are going to the seats reserved for the graduating class," Dad said, waved, and disappeared into the throng of people.

Zell pulled me behind a large oak tree that grew close by the parking lot.

"I have something I want to give you," he murmured drawing me close again.

"Zell, we need to go in," I argued pulling back.

"Not until you open this," he said in a trembling voice shoving a small, beautifully wrapped package in my hand. "This is your graduation gift from me."

I was taken aback. "Zell, no," I began sighing.

"Just open it," he growled. Hesitantly, I pulled the beautiful ribbons from the package and broke the taped end free. I pulled out a small box that had the name of the most expensive jeweler that I knew of in the Atlanta area.

I lifted the top of the box and gasped. There, nestled in the velveteen interior was the most dazzling ring I had ever seen. A very large diamond was nestled among a ring of sapphires, my birthstone, and other delicately cut smaller diamonds.

"Oh Zell, this is beautiful," I breathed. I touched the ring lovingly running my fingertips over the stones. Zell grasped my hand in his. With his other hand, he slipped it on the finger reserved for engagement and wedding rings. I held my hand out and admired the beauty of the ring. Then I began to take it off.

"I can't accept a gift like this, even from you," I sadly whispered.

"Don't be ridiculous," Zell huffed, and he grabbed me and pressed his lips to mine. Instantly, I became intoxicated with whatever power his kisses still held. My head began to reel with dizziness. I swayed, and he held me tight. "I love you, Annie. I have always loved you. For thousands of years, I have waited for you . . . loved you, and we had never met. Now that we are intricately in one another's lives, I never will live another day without you. Please love me back," Zell choked out in a voice filled with passion and emotion. I wish I could have spoken because for a brief moment, I was overcome with love for him. I would have told him right then for the first time that I loved him. I would have told him that there would never be another for me but him. But I could not speak. This was one time when Zell Starr's special gift would backfire on him. I could not make the words come. I was in a fog. I felt faint and closed my eyes. I did not see the look of hurt that crossed Zell's handsome face and darkened his silver eyes until they became as storm clouds.

Just then we were spotted by a camera crew, and they shouted my name. In a dead run, they headed for us. I heard Zell let out an exasperated sigh. He put the ring back on my finger, and he placed his arm around my shoulders and pulled me toward the lawn where chairs covered in white linen slip covers were placed waiting for us and the other graduates.

Bulbs flashed, reporters shoved microphones in my face shouting questions. Zell and I never stopped which was a good thing. I would have looked like a babbling fool. Zell hovered over me, shielding me from most of the ruckus. My head swam from Zell's kiss, the flashes of light, and reporters who were yelling at me. Zell guided me to my seat which being in alphabetical order was far from him. I knew that fact upset him. Jon was sitting in his seat only a few feet from me—Hayes, Hedrick, Hefner, Hemmingway, Holt, Howard. Zell stiffened when he saw him. I'm sure the smirk on Jon's face was meant for Zell.

Zell bent and kissed me just enough to the right of my lips not to send my head spinning again before he moved back ten rows to his seat. That kiss was meant for Jon to mull over. I was sure he kissed me just then to irritate him. I glanced in Jon's direction, and his face looked murderous. I could see the news crews moving their cameras into range to fix their lens on me. What I wouldn't give to be left totally alone: no news reporter, no cameras, no Jon, no Dark Ones. I thought back to the night at Zell's home. Was that really Jon, or was it just a dark creature taking on his appearance trying to persuade me to let him in?

My head began to clear, and I placed my cap on my head. Timidly, I turned around trying to find Zell in the sea of faces behind me. It was not that difficult as he towered over everyone in our class. I gave him a tremulous smile, and then I did something extraordinary. I blew him a kiss and smiled. It warmed my heart to see the expression on his face. I looked at the ring still on my finger. Then, I looked at him. He was watching me intently.

"Thank you," I whispered wishing he could hear me. I could tell he understood from the look on his face.

The mayor began to speak, and I tore my eyes from Zell's face and faced the podium. I began to daydream about tomorrow. My father gave me money and a vacation on the Mexican Rivera for a graduation present. Zell was going too, as my protector and friend. The three of us hoped the Dark Ones would not be aware that I had left the country. Zell reassured us that they are neither omnipotent nor omnipresent. Unless they were watching me 24/7, perhaps we could get away without their knowledge. My father was going to Zell's lake house for a mini-vacation. Zell talked him into spending the time while we were gone at the lake house, lest one of the Dark Angels become enraged when they cannot find me and try to get information from my father. Zell had made it Lionel's job in our absence to entertain and watch over my father. I exhaled a sigh of relief and tried to focus on the end of the mayor's speech. It seemed as if everything was set and everyone taken care of.

Principal Conley made a short speech, and then it was the Valedictorian's turn. After that speech ended, the giving of diplomas would begin. I closed my eyes and tried to imagine lying on the warm sand with the sun warming my face and Zell at my side. I could not wait. This time tomorrow we should be landing in Mexico. Zell scoffed at the idea of flying in a plane, but my father insisted. Of course, Zell gave in quickly not wanting to seem disrespectful. My father found a wonderful graduation gift for Zell. He commissioned an artisan make him a pair of cuff links crafted like beautiful silver wings. They were really striking, and I was glad my father loved Zell too. I commissioned the same craftsman to create a photo frame that resembled the cuff links. Then I enlarged a photo Dad had taken of Zell and me, and I mounted it in the winged frame. It really was striking. The wings of the frame seemed to fold around us as if protecting us. I knew Zell would love it. It seemed as if the three of us were bonding into a family. My father always wanted to include Zell in our plans, and Zell enjoyed my father's company. I loved them both with all my heart. Perhaps, I could find the words to tell Zell while we were in Mexico. I've never expressed love for any man but my father. I found it very difficult to do so now.

"Amy Adair," Ms. Howard called as Amy walked across the stage to receive her diploma from Principal

Conley. I jumped when I realized I had been daydreaming during the entire graduation ceremony so far. I noticed Ms. Howard looked especially pretty today. Ms. Howard sported a tanned complexion, dark eyes, and shoulder length sleek jet black hair. I really should introduce her to Lionel.

His wife died from cancer ten years ago. I asked Zell why he didn't use his blood to save Lionel's wife on the night we went to Saint Jude's. He said he offered to help her. She and Lionel had talked it over and decided to leave it in God's hands. She passed a few days later. I thought about them now. Lionel was so good to Zell. I wanted the best for him. I thought Lionel and Ms. Howard would make a striking couple. I was sure Lionel was here somewhere to watch Zell matriculate. After the ceremony, I would introduce them.

Suddenly, I felt tension in the atmosphere. I turned to see if I could read anything on Zell's face. I caught him searching the crowd—looking for something. Perhaps, he felt it too.

"Alexander Brown," Ms. Howard's voice took on the same monotone as in the classroom as she called out graduating student after graduating student. I decided she was really a cool person; she just needed some excitement in her life. She needed to step over into my world for a few hours. I laughed silently at the thought.

"Caitlyn Carnes," she announced. Caitlyn was a pretty brunette. I knew her, but we were not very close because she played in the band, a flute, I thought. I was an athlete, so we did not get many opportunities to interact. She would graduate and move on with her life. I know we could have been great friends. She was soft spoken, bright, and lovely. I think she was awarded a music scholarship from a university in Tennessee. I had a pang of regret that I would never see many of my classmates again. There was no one in the crowd that I did not like perhaps with the exception of Jon. Even though he betrayed me, I still harbored mixed feelings about him. I cared about him at one time. Even after the horrible things he had done, I still seemed unable to be mad at him. I never reported the kidnapping to the police. Zell talked to him. I don't know what Zell said to him. He probably said something to the effect that he would make sushi out of him if he ever came close to me again. Jon just gave me a creepy feeling now. I believe most of that feeling stems from the night at Zell's home when he or an imposter who looked like him stood on the porch speaking into the camera. Even now, when I think of that moment, I get the shivers.

"Dawson Dodd," Ms. Howard said as she smiled. She actually smiled! I couldn't believe it. I think that was the first time I had ever seen her smile. She had a dark mole on her face close to her lips that really made her look kind of sexy. She was dazzling when she smiled. She really should smile more often. Dawson was an outstanding history student, and for that reason, I think she was fond of him.

"Millicent Emerson," I tuned out Ms. Howard again as my thoughts drifted. Only two more rows of matriculating students, and it would be my turn. My uneasiness grew the closer I came to being called. I snuck a glance at Zell again, and he was ashen. His beautiful complexion was pasty. I think he was holding back on transforming because his face was stony and concentrated. His eyes were smoldering. He rose from his seat, He was only two seats in from the end of a row, ten rows behind me. I saw him slip from his seat and into the aisle. Very few people even noticed. In the back, I could see Lionel rise from his seat. What was up? I knew something was going on. I could feel it too.

It seemed as if a cloud of evil hovered overhead. I saw a television camera swing toward me. I let out a breath of air as though I had been exercising heavily. I turned again and searched for Zell. I could not see him anywhere. Anslie Harmond tapped my knee as she rose to line up at the end of the stage. I rose as if automated and stood. My knees wobbled. I was panting. Something was coming; I knew it. I moved robotically; although occasionally, I swayed from the panic I felt rising up in my chest. My breath caught in my throat as if I had been crying heavily. I would not cry. I would not. I willed myself to move and remain calm. Whatever was coming for me, I would deal with when it presented itself.

I reached the bottom of the stairs and waited. Anslie was standing in front of me waiting to be called. I looked at the sky that was beautiful and full of promise this morning, yet now it seemed ominous and foreboding. I swayed slightly, and my mind wandered. The day began as the perfect day to graduate from high school in an outside ceremony. Now, everything seemed menacing. Was it a good day to die? I shook my head at the morose thought which leaped into my mind.

"Anslie Harmond," Ms. Howard's voice washed over me like a cooling breeze. I was next. I waited and listened for my name to be called with my eyes closed. My thoughts roamed back to the island, and Zell and I were lying on a warm, sandy beach, laughing, talking, exhausted from swimming with the dolphins. I smiled.

"Anna Hayes," I hesitated for a moment immersed in the pleasant memory.

"Annie," Dr. Patty prompted from the top of the steps, "move."

I opened my eyes and moved up the few steps to the platform robotically. I could see television cameras behind the principal where she waited smiling. She was soaking up all this media attention, my diploma in her hand. I took a deep breath and stepped out on the stage. I smiled at the cameras, but stopped as I glanced around the audience. My heart jumped and caught in my throat. Panic gripped me and squeezed hard. They were everywhere just like the night at Zell's home. Dark Angels, tall and silent, possibly hundreds of them, stood darkly behind the parents, relatives, and friends who sat in the audience. Behind them, I could see dozens of hideous creatures waiting. People in the audience were oblivious to the menacing creatures standing darkly and silently behind them. I looked back toward the principal and the camera crew behind her. It seemed as if no one saw them but me. I looked back to the enormous, dark, winged figures. The Dark Ones stood tall and powerful in their angelic form. Some were in other forms, too hideous and frightening to look upon. I froze. Principal Conley looked uncomfortable and adjusted her suit jacket.

Ms. Howard looked irritated and called my name again. "Anna Hayes, please move forward to receive your diploma." I took a step forward again, but a dark winged figure moved behind the camera crew who stood behind Principal Conley. She was standing impatiently waving my diploma back and forth. I froze again horrified. I looked for an escape route, but there wasn't one. As I looked out over the audience, I knew the ring of Dark Angels would keep me from escaping. I began panting, my chest heaving with each breath. Then he came. He dropped out of the sky just as he had the first time we met except this time he was in his armor. He was magnificent, and when I saw him my heart melted. I ran for him. The audience gasped as he scooped me in his arms and gave a great thrust with his wings. We were barely ten feet off the ground when it felt as though we hit a brick wall. The Dark Angel from behind the film crew met us in the air, and the impact knocked me from Zell's grasp. I fell back to the wooden platform knocking the air from my lungs. As I lay there gasping, I saw Zell and the Dark Angel draw their swords. The battle was on.

The audience gasped again. Some stood up knocking over their chairs. Mothers gathered their small children to them. Most everyone was transfixed as the battle between Zell and the Dark Angel raged on overhead. Sparks flew from their swords and rained down upon my head, the heads of the people on the stage, and on those in the first few rows. I looked for my father. I could not see him, but I saw Lionel to the side, kneeling beside two, huge, black duffel bags. Matthew and Christopher were there, and I saw him put a sword in each of their hands. I looked back above me to see Zell twirl and sink his sword in the chest of the Dark Angel with both hands. The Dark One fell, breaking the boards of the platform when he hit. Zell was on him at once with his flaming sword drawn. He separated the Dark One's head from its body with one sword and sunk his flaming sword deep in its chest almost simultaneously.   No sooner was he done, than another angel came swooping at him, knocking him to the ground in front of the platform. Two hands grabbed at my arms dragging me to my feet. Matthew and Christopher were at my side guarding each flank. I could see Lionel coming up the steps toward me.

Zell and the second Dark Angel fought viciously. Their swords gave off deafening clanking sounds that left me unable to hear what Matthew and Christopher were shouting at one another. I had seen Zell fight many times, but never like this. He hammered away with hard, booming blows at the sword of the Dark Angel. He was fighting for our very lives, and we both knew it. I heard people in the audience screaming, knocking over chairs, looking for a way around the dark wall of creatures. I saw the television crew filming the ferocious fight. Fire flew from swords which clashed and rang. People in the audience caught sight of the Dark Angels and creatures. Screaming, then running, they panicked, but the Dark Creatures did not stop them. They, too, seemed absorbed in the fight between Zell and the Dark Angel. Zell stumbled and fell backward. The Dark Angel was on him instantly. Zell held up his sword to fend off the blow of his sword. Then something happened that charged the already electric atmosphere. Matthew left my side jumping to Zell's aide. He leaped through the air, and his sword came down on the Dark Angel slicing through its arm. The Angel crumpled at Zell's feet, and Matthew extended his hand to Zell. I almost laughed to see Matthew pull Zell to his feet. Zell towered over him when he was upright and back on his feet.

"Thank you my friend," Zell sighed, "but we may have started something by our actions." Even as he said that the Dark Ones moved from their self-appointed boundaries behind the now empty seats to circle the platform. Instantly, they closed in. Two Dark Angels bounded on the platform.

"Just as I feared," Zell said as he looked at Matthew. "The Dark Ones were waiting for this opportunity. You have entered the fight now, my friend."

"Bring it on," Matthew crowed at the two angels. Fear squeezed my heart. I knew Matthew was no match for the angels. I was sure Zell knew it too. The only one oblivious to the fact was Matthew. Zell would have to take them both on.

Magnificently, he twirled finishing the job Matthew started by separating the Dark Angel's head from his shoulders and simultaneously setting him alight with his flaming sword. It only took a second, and he was back with Matthew daring the Dark Angels to make the first move. He didn't wait long before the two angels jettisoned toward them. Zell knocked one from the platform, swinging his sword upward to counter a blow from the other. Matthew and Christopher both jumped over the edge of the platform onto the fallen Dark Angel. As if on cue, other guys from the senior class appeared. Some carried swords, and others carried ball bats, some metal chairs, and one a metal flag pole. They joined their friends, Matthew and Christopher, to fight the Dark One sprawled on the ground. The good thing about the living in the South is there are always plenty of good ol' boys who are always ready for a rumble. More friends of ours appeared armed with swords supplied I was sure by Lionel. It was a brawl now as a few more Dark Creatures moved in to help the downed Dark Angel.

I felt a touch on my arm and looked to find Jon standing there.

"Your new boyfriend duck out on you?" Jon smirked. Then he changed his tone and the smirk on his face changed to a look of concern. "Annie please don't be upset. I just want to help you. Let me get you out of here," Jon pleaded.

"Never. I'll never leave Zell," I ground out.

"If you don't, Zell will die. Matthew, Christopher, and other friends of ours will die too," Jon countered. "These things are after you, not Zell, not anyone but you. We get you away from here, and maybe this will stop. Look around. This is a life or death struggle. People are going to die. They will keep coming, and Zell and the others will keep fighting until they lose the battle. Have you seen how many there are?" Jon argued sweeping his hand around the panorama of the Dark Angels.

Jon was right. What he said made sense. Someone or maybe many people were going to die if I didn't get out of here. Could I live with the blood of my friends on my hands? I knew that I could not. I looked at Zell bravely fighting his third Dark Angel. There were hundreds of Dark Ones, just standing waiting to battle him. What if others dared to break the Covenant, enter into the war, and Zell had to fight multiple Dark Ones at a time? What if he grew exhausted after fighting dozens of them. I had to try to save him and my friends even if it meant that I would die. I would die for him. I would die for any of my friends. Had they not also made that decision when they entered into this brawl? Yes, I would die to save any of their lives. I made a decision. I reached for Jon's hand.

"Let's go then," I moaned.

Jon pulled me toward the back of the platform. We jumped to the ground. Crouching behind the platform, Jon pointed to his truck parked about 50 yards away.

"We'll run to my truck," he whispered.

Camera crews and reporters had not joined the other spectators and run. They were furiously filming the mayhem and reporting to the television audience. Police sirens could be heard in the distance. They would be here in mere minutes. Perhaps, we could escape in all the bedlam that was sure to break out when the police arrived.

Police cars began streaming in, east of the platform that we were hiding behind. Jon's truck was west. The reporters and camera crews were north. I began to be hopeful that we could reach his truck. My heart broke to leave Zell. I peered over the platform hoping to see him. He was fighting two Dark Angels. This was bad. Zell said that sending more than one Dark Creature at a time was forbidden. This meant that some Dark Ones were not honoring the Covenant. This knowledge sent a chill down my spine. Zell was a magnificent warrior, but he couldn't fight multiple evil creatures simultaneously. Other Dark Ones were still circling the stage waiting. Obviously, they were not sure about invoking the anger of the Archangels by breaking the Covenant. That was ours, mine and Zell's, only hope. Perhaps, the majority of the Dark Ones would not cross the line and enter into the fray.

We huddled and waited until the police began emerging from their vehicles. Then, we ran. I stumbled once and fell. After all, I was in dress shoes and a cap and gown. Jon came back for me and lifted me to my feet. I kicked off my shoes. I saw it when I turned for a last glimpse of Zell. One of the creatures spotted me and was bounding toward us.

"Run," I screamed. Jon looked past me to see what had set me off. I didn't have to tell him to run a second time. I run fast for a girl, but Jon passed me. He grabbed my hand as he ran past pulling me along even faster. I wanted to look over my shoulder, but I didn't dare. It was all I could do to maintain my balance as we ran with Jon pulling me along. A black SWAT team truck was pulling onto the road where Jon's truck was parked. They changed their route when they saw the Dark Creature chasing us and pulled their vehicle in between us and the Dark One. The SWAT team filed out of the truck pulling out weapons. They began firing at the Creature. The thing never even slowed. It took a great leap and cleared them and their vehicle. The SWAT team rolled around the vehicle still firing their weapons at the beast. One pulled a missile launcher from the vehicle, put the great Creature in his sights, and fired. The missile caught the creature in the backside. With a great roar, it buckled to its knees and flipped end over end for several revolutions. I knew it wouldn't stay down long if they didn't sever its head from its body. I jerked my hand loose from Jon's and ran back toward them. A few of them ran to meet me.

"You have to cut off its head, or it will regenerate. It's an eternal creature. Its body will heal, and you'll have to deal with him again if you don't separate its head from its body," I gasped breathing heavily emphasizing the separating its head from its body.

"What?" A young officer asked, puzzled.

"Look around you," I yelled.

"This isn't your everyday freak show. These are supernatural creatures. They are not dead until their head is separated from their body no matter how dead they look or how serious they are injured. You have to cut off their head!" Even as I said it, the Dark Creature moved into the background. All eyes were looking at me oblivious to the movements of the creature, but I was watching the Creature.

With a menacing growl, it tried to stand on its feet. The entire SWAT team turned around as one. Fire burst from their weapons. They did not stop firing until their weapons were empty, and the Dark Creature dropped to the ground once again. "Cut off its head," I yelled, breaking into sobs.

The officer that I had just been talking to ran to the side of the Creature and pulled his knife. He grabbed the hilt with both hands and plunged the knife deep in the Dark One's neck. Blood spurted all over him. He wiped the creature's blood from his eyes and sawed at the neck with his knife until the head was released from the body.

"Now, burn it," I shouted still sobbing and trembling.

"Now Mam, There is no way that the animal is getting up. Roasting the thing isn't necessary. Actually, I think it's against fire code to start a blaze here."

I moved to the officer and put my face in his face. "I'm Annie. That is The Anak," I said through clenched teeth pointing to where Zell was fighting like the amazing, supernatural warrior that he is. "and that," I ground out, "is no animal. He," I pointed to where Zell was in a life and death struggle against two Dark Angels, "always burns them after taking off their head. He says that burning them is the only way to finish them for good."

The officer looked from me to Zell and back again several times. Then he shouted, "Someone build a bonfire with that thing."

Jon grabbed my hand and tugged. Hesitantly, I moved with him, but my eyes watched Zell. The thought that I may never see Zell again crossed my mind.

My body shuddered, and I felt faint. Jon put his arm tenderly around my shoulder. "Annie come, we have to go." Still watching Zell over my shoulder, I moved to go with him.

We ran for his truck. We were only twenty feet from his truck when Jon stopped. I was still trying to run and watch Zell, and I ran smack into Jon's back when he abruptly came to a halt. I looked at him, puzzled. Following his gaze, I allowed my eyes to go in the direction that he was staring. It was him! The one Zell had been talking to in my dream or in reality which is what I was beginning to suspect. He stood on the hood of Jon's truck. Jon pushed me behind him. Slowly, we began to back up. Regardless of who he was, he was the most magnificent looking creature I had ever seen in real life, in the movies, or in fantasy pictures. He was a giant of light. His enormous wings were only tipped in black, but it outlined the silhouette of his wings beautifully. His handsome face dazzled me. Every perfect feature shone with an eternal light softening his chiseled features. He was mesmerizing; it was almost impossible to turn my gaze from him. The being jumped from the hood of Jon's truck to land only a few feet in front of us. We turned to run, but It was faster. Suddenly, It was in front of us again.

"Where are you going, Annie?" It asked.

"Away from here," I answered.

"But why? This is a lovely graduation party, don't you think?" It asked contemptuously.

"No, I don't think this is a party. I think it is a massacre," I answered, feeling the anger rising in me.

"You can put an end to it all," the being offered.

"Who are you?"

"I believe you know who I am."

"Are you Zell's father, Azâzêl?"

"None other," he answered, spreading his arms wide. His mouth spread into a gleaming, beautiful smile just as wide. Instead of being a warm smile though, it was an evil smile that chilled my blood.

"Zell will kill you if you hurt me," I argued.

"My dear, you think Zâzêl would kill his own father for a human girl?" Azâzêl smiled again spreading his hands wide as if asking a question and raised one finely arched eyebrow.

"Yes, yes, he would kill you to save me," I sputtered the words at him.

"Zell may try to kill me, but he will never succeed. He will only end up dying himself. Is that what you want?"

"Of course not. I love him."

"Ah yes, true human love. How quaint it is that you both feel love for one another, a lowly human girl and an Annunaki, the son of an immortal angel."

"Have you never loved anyone? Zell's mother, didn't you love her?"

Azâzêl threw back his head and laughed. The laughter was anything but lighthearted. It sounded menacing and evil. Abruptly, he stopped and looked at me. "Love a human? Only Zâzêl is weak enough to love humans. I only use them for whatever it is that I desire at the moment. Then, I usually dispose of them. However, Zell's mother was exceptional. She was the most beautiful human that was ever created." Despite his words, I could see his face change and soften as he spoke of Zell's mother. "Her only downfall was that she was so good, so noble, and so righteous," he continued curling his nose up at the memory. "But then, that is part of the reason she was so attractive to me. It's not as much fun spoiling someone not as noble as she."

"Look, Mr. Dark Angel," Jon began, "just let Annie and I go. I promise you that she will not see Zell again." Jon was silenced when Azâzêl turned his cold, dark stare on him.

"Do not speak to me again, or I will send your dark soul where it belongs," Azâzêl growled.

"You'll do no such thing. Jon is not involved in all this," I interrupted.

"I told you before that you can put an end to it all." Azâzêl turned his dark stare back to me.

"Sorry, but I'm needed here," I smirked, not knowing where the bravery or stupidity was coming from to stand up to this fearsome angelic being.

"Run to the truck, Annie," Jon whispered, putting his truck keys in my hand. Jon stepped in front of me to face Azâzêl, and I blindly did as I was told darting off to the side headed for Jon's truck. The sound of steel sliding from a steel sheath stopped me in my tracks. I turned in time to see Azâzêl thrust his gleaming sword deep into Jon's chest. Whatever Jon had done to me in the past was forgiven by his bravery and self-sacrifice of the last few minutes.

"No," I screamed and ran back to Jon's side.

Christopher and Matthew joined me there and began taunting Azâzêl with words and swords. A couple of the Swat Team officers arrived and began firing at the gigantic angel. If Azâzêl had not had such a black heart, I would have admired the way he fended off the bullets with his sword and his wings. His agility and abilities were clearly not of this world. He pulled two daggers from his belt and threw one at Matthew. With a deadly thud, the dagger found its mark in his chest. The other landed in the neck of a young officer just above where his bulletproof vest stopped. With a gurgling sound, the young man slumped to the ground. Azâzêl acted at once and was on the other officer in the blink of an eye. I groaned as I recognized the other young man as the one I had told to cut off the head of the Dark Beast earlier.

"Stop," I sobbed, but it was too late. Azâzêl thrust his sword up to the hilt through the bulletproof vest with inhuman strength until most of the sword was protruding from the officer's back. "No, no, no," I sobbed again, "please stop."

"He's dead Annie. Matthew's dead," Christopher cried out. Horror darkened his youthful countenance. He was kneeling on the ground with Matthew cradled in his arms. He held up a hand covered in Matthew's blood as he spoke to me.

Azâzêl turned to me and grinned menacingly, "He's dead, Annie. Matthew's dead," he said mocking Christopher. "All out of heroes, Annie?" I could see network camera crews filming the whole scene in the background behind Azâzêl.

"Actually, father, no, she has one hero left," Zell remarked coolly stepping between his father and me.

"Zâzêl leave us. This is between the girl and me," Azâzêl coaxed.

"No, father, whatever concerns Annie, concerns me," Zell countered.

"I don't want to kill you, son," Azâzêl's voice seemed to plead with him.

"Then don't. Leave here," Zell reasoned with him.

"I can't do that. This is bigger than you or me. She is going to give mankind hope," Azâzêl accused.

"What a great crime that is," Zell laughed sarcastically.

"She has already done irreparable damage," Azâzêl lamented.

"How is that?" Zell asked.

"*They*," Azâzêl shrieked, and he made a great sweeping motion indicating the crowd of spectators, the media, and the police all standing, watching as this drama played itself out, "*know*."

"*They know*? I don't follow you, father," Zell answered, sounding as confused as I felt.

"Yes, before this, this generation's faith had waned. We were but fairy tales in an ancient book. Look at this spectacle! The camera, the witnesses! Now, *they know* the truth. Humankind now knows that if *I exist*, if *you exist*, then *He exists*."

"Is the truth so bad then, father?" Zell asked softly — innocently.

"I left Him and the splendors of His world and followed another because I was jealous of the love he gave to these lowly humans, jealous of *Him*, *His truth*, and *His love*. Then, this wee bit of flesh exposes the whole world to the truth of our existence and His. Doubt is gone. Disbelief is gone. Look around you. These people know that death is not the end now. How can you argue mortality, living for the gratifications of now, living selfishly, when before your very eyes you see the evidence of immortality?" Azâzêl grieved, his voice ending in a thunderous roar.

Most of the Dark Ones had left. I guessed they knew when they had crossed the line and wanted to be gone from the scene. Only a few Dark Angels stood in the distance watching this spectacle. I dropped to my knees in front of Jon, Matthew, and the young officers and wept.

"This is all my fault. I'm not worth their sacrifice."

"Annie, your message is well worth their sacrifice." Zell stated moving to kneel next to Matthew.

"What message? I haven't said or done anything worthwhile. I've only managed to get people murdered," I cried.

"Annie, do have any doubt now that you mother lives on? Do you still doubt the existence of an Eternal One?"

"No, I can honestly say that I don't doubt anymore. I believe now."

"Then, you can help them," Zell drew me close and whispered in my ear tenderly.

"How?" I asked as I choked back great sobs.

"You know, Saint Jude's Hospital. It didn't have to be my blood Annie. My blood is now your blood," Zell whispered privately. Leaning over, he stroked my hair and handed me the hilt of his sword. "Just a small cut will do."

I blinked several times, mulling over what Zell was saying. Then, as if a light bulb went off, I smiled slightly and my face lit up. "Yes," I nodded, smiling sweetly at Zell.

"What are you doing?" Azâzêl thundered as I turned Zell's sword against my forearm and cut an inch of flesh. Zell leaned over hiding my actions from the crowd of spectators. I leaned over Jon's wound and let the drops of blood seep into the deep gash. Then I turned to Matthew, dropped to my knees, and cradled him in my arms rocking him gently back and forth.

"Matthew, Matthew, you were so brave and loyal. I'm sorry that I did this to you," I cried over him until I was exhausted. Many of the people in the crowd were weeping with me. Gently, as I held him, I rubbed my cut, dripping arm over his wounds. Great drops of my blood mixed with his blood and into his wound. Gently, I hugged him to me, kissed his cheek, and lowered him onto the soft grass.

I moved to the first Swat Team officer.

"Thank you," I whispered, trying to hide my actions from the crowd of onlookers and the camera crews. The scene was chaos, and hopefully, no one would notice what I was secretly trying to accomplish.

Finally, I tore open the shirt of the officer that had been in charge of the SWAT team and tugged at the torn bulletproof vest which had been no match for Azâzêl's supernatural strength and razor sharp sword. I freed the officer from his vest. Sitting on my knees and holding the officer with his back to me in an embrace, I crisscrossed my arms across the large, jagged laceration in the officer's chest. I hoped most everyone's attention was focused on Zell and Azâzêl as I rubbed my cut, bleeding arm over his wound.

"You know she was running away with him," Azâzêl alleged.

I lifted my eyes in time to see a great sadness descend upon Zell's countenance. He looked into my eyes, and then he glanced at Jon and back to my eyes again. I could see tears glittering behind his lashes, but he would not allow them to fall.

"Were you leaving with him, Annie?" Zell asked sadly.

"Yes, but . . . ," I whispered and gently placed the officer on the ground. I rose to plead with Zell.

"Ha, you see the harlot admits it," Azâzêl incriminated and lunged at my chest with his glittering sword. It was as if time slowed. I saw the sun reflecting brilliantly off Azâzêl's sword as it plunged through empty space toward its target—me. I braced to meet the attack, leaving the young officer at my feet, blood dripping down my arm, my fingers, and on to the young man's chest. I slowly closed my eyes as I waited for the sword to meet its target—my heart.

I thought, "What did it matter? Zell thinks I have betrayed him with Jon. He thinks I was running away and leaving him as he was fighting for our lives. My heart was already broken that Zell may think I had betrayed him. What more could a sword to the heart do, but go ahead and put me out of my misery?"

I watched the sword racing toward me, but I was not afraid. Not only had Zell protected me since my birth, but he restored the faith I had lost at the death of my mother. I'm going to join her; I calmly thought. Time seemed to cease to exist as I thought of the vision I had of my mother in the hospital, and as I thought of all the happy, exciting, and frightening times that I had shared with Zell, my friends, and my father. I didn't want to leave any of them, but I was confident that my mother was waiting on the other side. I closed my eyes and waited for the impact.

Then, he stepped in front of me and took the impalement meant for me. He was facing me. I saw the sword ease slowly out of his armor in the front. Instead of me, Azâzêl had pierced Zell through the back. The death that was meant for me, Zell willing took. Even though he always believed in his heart that an afterlife for one such as he was sure to be suffering beyond description, he chose death in my place. I was splattered and covered in Zell's blood.

"Noooo," Azâzêl gave a great roar when he realized what had happened. "Not him," he uttered in a great moaning voice.

"I love you, Annie. I will always love you. My one wish is that you could have loved me too," Zell whispered to me only inches from my face before his beautiful silver eyes lost their shimmer and became the unseeing eyes of the dead. He slumped to his knees. I threw my arms around him to hold him up as Azâzêl's sword exited back out of his body.

"I love you, too," I sobbed. "Don't go. Please come back to me. You are my first love, my last love, and my only love. I don't want to live without you either. I love you. I love you. I love you. I'm sorry that I could never tell you." I pressed kisses against his forehead and the top of his head repeatedly as I struggled to hold the great weight of him up.

"You witch. I'm going to send you to hell with him," Azâzêl screamed in a deafening roar leaning his head back and screaming profanities into the sky. The crowd of onlookers behind me started to nervously inch backward.

"Neither of us are going to hell today," I whispered as I remembered Zell's sword that I still held in my hand, my actions hidden from Azâzêl by Zell's body. Letting Zell's body tumble from my arms, I leaped and plunged the sword through Azâzêl's cold, cold heart as he stood, arms outstretched, still threatening the heavens with his curses. A look of shock crossed his face as he realized he had been wounded by a "wee bit of human flesh."

I returned to Zell and tenderly gathered him in my arms. I sunk to my knees under the weight of Zell's limp body. Lovingly, I turned Zell's lifeless body over withdrawing the flaming sword from its sheath.

"Give the sword to me Annie. I'll finish him off," I heard Kate's voice as if miles away. Kate was there resplendent and shining in her transformation. She had been fighting with Zell as he fought the Dark Angels. She was bloody and looked incredibly weary. I imagined she had been fighting alongside Zell while I was running away with Jon. Guilt washed over me. I made a whimpering sound and handed the sword to Kate. Kate took me in her arms while I wept.

I heard a gasp from the crowd of spectators and film crews who had stood silently by mesmerized by the scene unfolding before them. Before Azâzêl could be finished off, the whole sky lit up with an intensity that was blinding. I shielded my eyes. When I could focus again, there were three great angels of light standing before me.

"Peace be unto you," the one closest to me said.

"There can be no peace for me. Zell, the Last of the Annunaki, is dead, and it's all my fault," I answered stonily. "Who are you? Have you come to kill me too?"

The second angel smiled and rested his hand on my shoulder, "There has been enough bloodshed today, Anna. I am Gabriel. That is Michael," he said, motioning to the first angel that spoke to me, "and our brother is Rafael. We are the Archangels of Heaven, who stand watch over humanity. We have come to take Azâzêl back to Torment."

Wearily, I gazed at them. They were beyond description. The love they emanated was palpable.

"Please, make sure he doesn't escape this time," I asked quietly.

The three angels smiled. I thought I heard them laughing, but perhaps it was just the wind in the trees as the bright light of their presence faded. They took Azâzêl's limp body, held firmly in the grasp of Gabriel and Rafael, with them as they faded.

I saw Matthew's chest heave from the corner of my eye, and I returned to his side.

"Hey kiddo, what happened?" Matthew croaked weakly.

"You were amazing. That's what happened," I smiled, hugging Matthew to me tears flowing again. "Thank you, Matthew. You are a loyal friend to Zell and me. I want to thank you too, Christopher. We could not have asked for better friends," I choked out squeezing Christopher's hand and giving Matthew another hug.

"Seriously? I was amazing?"

"Hey man, you were dead," Christopher whispered reverently.

"Did you get that?" I heard a reporter ask a cameraman. "She brought him back to life."

I heard Jon and the Swat Team officer groan, and I moved to check on them. I helped each one get up as I heard the crowd gasp.

"She healed them too," loud shouts came from the crowd.

"It's a miracle from heaven," another said.

"She's a prophet!" A man shouted dropping to his knees.

"I'm not a prophet," I answered. "I'm just Annie."

I tuned all of them out, and I returned to Zell's side. I rolled him over and cradled him in my arms. I helped the others, but I knew somehow it was not within my power to help the one I loved. He was neither human nor an angel. He had killed the other Annunaki, so I knew that I could not bring him back. The one who's first and only thought was to protect me even until death. I cried over him and rocked him in my arms as a mother does her babe. I whispered quiet words of love in his ear. The rest of the world blurred. The only reality for me was Zell lying dead in my arms.

Dad, Lionel, and Ms. Howard were suddenly at my side.

"I'm sorry, honey. I loved him too," Dad murmured as he slipped one arm around my shoulder and the other around Zell's shoulder. I sobbed and clutched Zell's lifeless body closer to me. I could see the news crews moving in for a shot, and I buried my face against Zell's lovely, lifeless one. My heart broke in two as I tried to muffle the great wail rising in my chest from escaping my lips. I wept and sobbed into Zell's hair hiding my face from the cameras.

Lionel and Ms. Howard stood silently side by side. Lionel put his hand on Dad's shoulder, and Ms. Howard silently stroked my hair. Paramedics arrived on the scene and checked Jonny, Matthew, and the two officers. They tried to take Zell from my arms, but I cried out and held on tightly. Rocking him back and forth, I sobbed uncontrollably, great tears splashing on Zell's hair, face, and arms. Through my tears, I could see a growing, gawking crowd of onlookers and the media encircling us, yet they were standing reverently watching and sharing my grief. The Swat Team had removed their helmets, and the cameramen removed their ball caps. I could see some people with their heads bowed crying shamelessly with me. I didn't care. I wanted to die, too. I didn't deserve Zell. He was a much better person than I was. This young man claimed to be only half human, yet his humanity was his very essence. The anguish I felt in my heart would never be quenched. First, my mother and now Zell lay in death's grip in my arms. He had ravished my heart, and I knew that my life would never be the same. I should have died instead of Zell.

"I should have died. It should have been me." I cried.

"Annie, Master Zâzêl would never have allowed you to perish."

"It should have been me. His father meant to kill me."

With my father on one side and Lionel on the other, they lifted me to my feet. As members of the Swat team surrounded Zell and prepared to take him to the morgue, I broke free from my father and Lionel throwing myself upon his chest and kissing his lips before my love left me forever. The Taser-like effect was gone. I did not tremble or shake. He was gone. My friend, my love, my heart, and my life was gone.

Final Release in the Anak Trilogy

Coming

Summer, 2015

1.HEARTBREAK

THE ANNUNAKI WAS MUCH TOO LARGE FOR AN ambulance. It took ten Swat team members to lift Zell's body into a tractor trailer that the police called to transport him to the morgue and five people to hold me back. Much to my relief, he had not transformed back to my Zell, my love with the silver eyes. He had remained as the final Annunaki. Somehow, it was easier for me. I don't think I could have stood the pain if he had not stayed as the Anak. I tore away from all the hands that held me and ran after him. The Swat Team had just bolted the door and would not open it again.

"Don't go. Come back to me. Don't go on without me. We could have done so much more." This pain of departing tore at me. I screamed beating on the door. I wanted to scream out his name over and over, but even though he was dead, I wanted to protect his identity.

Dad put his arm around me and drew me away from the trailer. Slowly, I was guided by Dad, Lionel, and Ms. Howard to Zell's car. Conversation swirled around me, but I could not focus on whom was speaking, nor on what they were saying. My dad asked the medic to give me a sedative, but I was comatose long before it took effect. I didn't speak nor respond when others spoke to me. As if all that remained was a ghostly shell of myself, I allowed myself to be placed tenderly in Zell's vehicle.

"Mr. Hayes, I think you and Annie should stay at the lake house tonight. I know it will be hard for Miss Annie to be there, but I fear for her safety. I don't know if the Dark Ones have called off the hunt, but I don't think we should take chances until we are sure. We can go by your home, and you can pack a bag."

"Yes, Lionel, I think that is a good idea—until we're sure."

When we pulled in the drive at Zell's lovely home, I began to weep again. I could not believe Zell was gone. I could not believe he would not come through the door to greet me. I could not believe that I would never see him again. I could not believe that I would wake from my nightmares, and he would not be there to comfort me. It was too much to bear.

While Dad and Lionel carried a couple of bags in the house, I wandered into Zell's room and into his closet. I found two shirts sitting on a chair that were headed for the laundry. I gathered them in my arms and buried my face in them. My legs gave way, and I slipped into a heap in agony on the floor. I never thought my capacity for love was this deep, nor my ability to feel pain so vast. I buried my face further into his shirts and wept.

That was the way Dad and Lionel found me.

ABOUT THE AUTHOR

Sherry Fortner received her undergraduate degree in Education from the University of Tennessee and her Masters and Educational Specialist degrees from Lincoln Memorial University. A retired schoolteacher, she now writes romance and paranormal novels fulltime from her home in Southeastern Tennessee where she lives with husband, Ray, her five horses, four Yorkshire Terriers, a barn cat, and assorted chickens. *Forever Girl* is her second release in the Anak Trilogy. When not writing, Sherry can be found outside in her garden, riding around her ranch, or spending time with her children, grandchildren, and animals. Visit Sherry at her website sherryfortner.com .

www.ingramcontent.com/pod-product-compliance
Lightning Source LLC
Chambersburg PA
CBHW070839120626
46556CB00002B/810